DEATH AND SEVEN

DAN WELCH

Janet,
With whom I lost my rookie standing!

I'll never forgot January of 2017.

Best wishes &
Dan

Appropriate for Teens, Intriguing to Adults

Immortal Works LLC
1505 Glenrose Drive
Salt Lake City, Utah 84104
Tel: (385) 202-0116

© 2018 Dan Welch

Cover Art by Mackenzie Seidel
mackenzieseidel.weebly.com

Formatted by FireDrake Designs
www.firedrakedesigns.com

All rights reserved, including the right to reproduce this book or portions thereof in any form whatsoever. For more information email contact@immortal-works.com or visit www.immortal-works.com/contact

ISBN 978-0-9990205-8-6 (Paperback)
AISN B07F5FTWK1 (Kindle Edition)

to Carol Ann Irish

CHAPTER 1

Amanda Wilson was not actively religious nor given to superstition. She did not consult with angels, believe in UFO abductions nor consider herself reincarnated. Neither, however, was she unaffected by the talking dead.

The corpse, propped up in a bed ten feet away, was slightly green and vaguely smelly.

Amanda had not initially recognized the electronically generated monotone she heard as speech and it took her a moment to associate the "voice" with the corpse.

"Ben I fab bafus faddy . . . womaz suffell . . . shed." The voice trailed off.

Dr. Kenneth Conklin monitored the flickering lights and gauges of the equipment wired to the corpse while Dr. Gregory Ellerby, poised at a microphone, conducted the apparent interrogation. They were unaware that Amanda, struggling to control herself, was crouching in the doorway of the dimly lit laboratory.

"Want me to jolt him?" asked Kenny Conklin, a small, round man with long dark hair and a full beard. He made Amanda think of some forest creature in a lab coat.

"Not just yet," said Dr. Ellerby. He leaned forward in his chair, keyed the microphone on his desk and asked, "What did Mrs. Russell say on that Friday you had breakfast with her?"

There was no movement of the corpse or animation in the dead man's face but the voice resumed, "Seato mat red pot woont bissued nilt mond."

That seemed to please Ellerby. He made some notes and then asked a follow-up question. "At breakfast that Friday, did Mrs. Russell say how she knew the report would not be released until the following Monday?"

When the corpse didn't answer Kenny Conklin said, "Come on, Greg. We need to keep this moving."

Ellerby repeated the question. When the corpse still didn't answer, he nodded and Kenny hit a switch. Sparks flew from the machinery and electricity cracked and popped. A twisted pathetic moan came from the dead man. Amanda cried out in sympathy.

Startled, Greg and Kenny got to their feet and rounded on her. She straightened up, holding her hands instinctively in front of her, moving backwards slowly. "I'm sorry," she said. "I'm sorry . . . it was open." She bent down and picked up a large foam dart from the floor. "This was stuck in the door, keeping it open. I need to talk to one of you."

Greg and Kenny stopped moving forward.

"I need a signature for the second heart-lung unit," she continued, "a signature for the requisition."

That was true. She was the office admin, the entire office administrative staff, in fact, including receptionist in the small lobby where she spent her days behind her orderly desk almost totally undisturbed. "The mail pickup comes just before lunch. I wanted to get it out today."

Greg Ellerby, who was tall and smiled easily, who Amanda thought was cute as opposed to his creepy little friend Dr. Conklin, shrugged his shoulders. "Yeah." He motioned to his right, toward the end of the room where there were chairs and a smart board. "We've been talking about your role here. Do you have time to chat a bit?"

Amanda had loads of time. She had time to mull over her decision to leave Washington for a job at this VA research facility in upstate New York, her brief marriage which had gone so listlessly and expensively wrong, and the drab expanse of the rest of her young life stretching before her. But having loads of free time was not information you shared with the boss. She looked at her watch and made something of a pout with her small, neat mouth. "Okay."

Greg Ellerby spread his arms to encompass the room. "I guess this all looks pretty weird to you?"

Amanda said it certainly did.

"It's all legal," said Kenny. "It's legal, but it's secret . . . really secret."

"I have a very good security clearance," said Amanda.

Greg nodded. "The problem is that this is an investigation and some of the people we're investigating are inside government. They have good security clearances too." He paused before continuing.

"Normally," he said with his eyes locked on hers, "in a situation like this you would be detained."

Amanda understood the subtle threat but smiled reflexively.

He continued. "Kenny and I have been talking about working something out with you. We really do need help and including you in our operation is a pretty easy way to get some. We know you now, you're obviously competent and conscientious. And you do have a very good security clearance."

Amanda looked over Greg's shoulder at the corpse. The dead man, a Caucasian and a senior citizen, nude at least to the waist and greener than she had first realized, had restraints on his wrists.

"We have," Greg said. "Dr. Conklin and I . . . we have a little medical device company, Glimmer Development, and we've been working on artificial cranial nerves." He waited a moment, smiled again, and then continued. "Most nerves go down the spinal column from the brain. But the cranial nerves handle stuff that's inside the head, like seeing and hearing."

Amanda nodded.

Greg continued. "Implanting the nerves is very sensitive surgery. We got some cadavers to work out the technique. They're powered."

"What's powered?" asked Amanda warily.

"The nerves," he said. "They have tiny fuel cells in them.

"The brain runs on very low currents but we didn't realize how low. Even our tiny currents were too high and when we put them in the dead brain, they started causing reactions."

When she made no sign, he went on. "It's like when you start your car and it doesn't start. The starter motor is turning the engine over and a lot of the stuff in the engine is working: the cylinders are going up and down, the valves are opening and closing, the spark plugs are firing, but the engine is not really running." When Amanda still made no sign, Greg smiled.

"We discovered that we could interrogate the corpse," said Kenny. "The bones and membranes in the ear still work, so there is input signal, and we run that down one of our artificial nerves. That pumps electricity into the brain. We have an artificial voice box on the output nerves and we use a heart-lung machine and a port for liquid nutrition."

Kenny paused a moment, looking at Amanda. Apparently satisfied, he continued, "There are no psychological defense mechanisms in the dead person. The corpse will tell you anything you want to know. It's like accessing a database."

Greg interrupted. "One guy we got was a government employee—a crooked government employee. We got all this detailed information about various shenanigans. We were about broke and, since the stuff involved government fraud, we submitted it to a whistleblower program. We started getting paid. Then a couple of guys from the whistleblower program came around, wondering about our sources and, given that they were federal investigators and we had a fresh corpse in the lab, we explained. They came back in about a week and made us an offer."

"This man," he said, indicating the corpse, "is . . . *was* . . . Norbert Wickliffe. He was executed for treason. He's dead but his head is still full of information, information about financial fraud and criminal manipulation of the markets."

A couple of pennies dropped for Amanda. The effort to clean up Wall Street had had pretty amazing results since financial malfeasance at institutions considered too big to fail started to be prosecuted as treason. There were a lot of convictions, a fair number of executions, and the rats seemed to be ratting each other out pretty regularly. Money was coming back into the markets with public trust in the institutions and, for the most part, people were delighted. A rich source of inside information would explain a lot about the success of prosecutions.

Amanda was interested.

CHAPTER 2

"We find . . ." The jury foreman looked down at the notes in his hand.

Sarah Russell gripped Andy Crane's arm with both hands. He turned to console her but his eyes fell into her deep and artfully displayed cleavage. Embarrassed, he turned away quickly.

She had small children, and he had tried to convince her to dress down and dumpy, to play the embattled young mother. Instead, she stood motionless atop four-inch heels, sheathed in designer fashion and posed for a magazine cover.

". . . guilty on all counts," the foreman said.

Sarah Russell's grip tightened. A noticeable gasp escaped the gallery. Andy affected what he thought was an appropriate expression and patted her arm. In fact, he had expected the verdict. It was pretty clear from the evidence that she'd done it.

"Guess we're going to have to make a deal," she said grimly.

He had tried to explain to her that the time to make a deal was before you were convicted, but she had been adamant, convinced, he thought, that former associates would not testify against her or that some backroom magic would be worked if she kept her mouth shut.

Judge Hardt gaveled for attention and called out Sarah Russell by name. "You've been found guilty of treason. Do you understand?"

"Yes," she replied.

The judge turned to the prosecutor. "What do the feds want here?"

"Death and seven," replied Zeke Keele, the burly young man representing the government.

Sarah Russell got quiet as she sometimes did. She was extremely bright and Andy assumed she was deep in thought. Judge Hardt addressed her again, restating that she had been convicted on two counts of treason. He set the sentencing hearing for the following week. Then he turned to Zeke Keele. "I want to be absolutely clear here, these are capital offenses. Your office is formally calling for the death penalty?"

"Yes, Your Honor," replied Zeke. "Death and seven."

Treason law allowed for the seizure of a traitor's property but it could only be held until the traitor's death. By holding the body for seven years after execution the government essentially prevented the person's being declared dead under civil law and could thus hold the perpetrator's property for seven years. Seized property included electronic records of business and financial transactions and with seven years and ever advancing technology, federal investigators could sift and grind through those records with unremitting precision.

Andy turned from Sarah and saw her sister Martha sitting, as usual, directly behind the defense. Sarah's husband, Frank Russell, sat with Martha. Frank had been supportive throughout the trial though both he and Sarah maintained that he had been blindsided by the charges against her.

Andy exchanged a sympathetic and concerned glance with Martha and Frank and crossed no-man's-land to the prosecutor's table and Zeke Keele. The courtroom was not crowded, but Andy Crane, tall and lanky and wearing his trademark pearl gray suit, attracted attention from the gallery.

When prosecutors had first carried the argument that malfeasance at financial institutions deemed "too big to fail" constituted a threat to the nation and was therefore treason, there had been a lot of interest in the trials. Now there was only a small cluster of journalists and cognoscenti in attendance along with a smattering of aspiring attorneys, the latter there to see how the big money was made.

"We'd like some time to talk deal," Crane said.

Zeke seemed amused. "She's ready to deal . . . now?"

"As her attorney, I need to see what can be done."

"So she's not really ready?"

"It's going to be a busy few days," said Andy. "We're allowed one appeal and we have to get ready for the sentencing hearing in a week. I want to be sure that somewhere in there your office and mine have a chance to see if we might reach some sort of arrangement."

"You made us go to trial, Andy," said Zeke. "That cost us a lot of time and money."

"You're asking the court to kill her," replied Andy.

The two men had known each other since middle school in Connecticut. They had taken different paths to the Manhattan South Federal Courthouse, but they had been and still were friends. Zeke took the barb, discontinued his lecture on the protocols of deal-making, and set up an appointment.

CHAPTER
3

A sharp and persistent beep woke Amanda and she sat up in bed. She did not know where she was.

She heard muffled voices somewhere near, men's voices. She was shaking. She wore only light pajamas and underwear and she wrapped her arms around herself protectively.

Slowly she made out details of the room in the half light and recognized the vague voices as Greg's and Kenny's. The beeping had probably come from some monitoring equipment in the lab.

Then, with a pang of remorse and foreboding, she remembered that she'd moved into one of the patient rooms on the Glimmer ward.

Greg and Kenny had convinced her that, at least in the short term, she needed to stay in the facility. There were, they said, security issues, and they actually did need her twenty-four-seven. They were willing to pay quite a lot for her services. But in retrospect, in the dark, her decision to move in seemed foolish and reckless.

She needed to go to the bathroom, but she resisted for a few minutes. Finally she got up. Her bare feet felt the chill of the tile floor. She took a thin robe from her bedside chair and pulled it on over her pajamas.

A dim nightlight glowed in the bathroom and she felt better when she saw the collection of things she had brought from home. She and

Greg, Dr. Ellerby, had gone to her apartment to pick up clothes and personal supplies and clean out the refrigerator. They had also gone to the post office where she rented a box to forward her mail to. When that was done they went to lunch.

The restaurant on the other side of town had a fresh, local, and expensive cuisine. Amanda always took extra efforts with her appearance and once again she was thankful that she did. Heads turned discreetly when she and Greg came into the dining room. They made an attractive couple.

Greg was genuinely excited about the company, Glimmer Development, and he seemed to really enjoy talking about it with someone other than Dr. Conklin.

Glimmer's government client thought the technology would remain classified for the foreseeable future. At some point it would be made an official clandestine operation. It would go on the black budgets and be presented in secret to congressional oversight committees. When that happened, Drs. Ellerby and Conklin would hand the interrogation technology off and go back to private life and the artificial nerve business.

"But right now there are only a handful of people who even know this technology exists. The government guys we're working with . . ." Greg leaned forward and whispered with a hint of amusement, "Kenny calls them the cabal."

He straightened up and continued, "Anyway, those guys have us tucked away in the veterans' hospital as a sort of skunk works project. We're classified as a contract organization and we get whatever we ask for. Nobody ever comes around asking questions. So . . ."

A waitress came with a carafe of ice water and Greg ordered wine. The attractive waitress went unnoticed by Greg. His attention remained firmly fixed on Amanda.

"So?" asked Amanda when the waitress had gone.

"So," he said, "for now we are in the law enforcement business."

"And that seems to be going well." She smiled.

"It works for our development," he conceded. "Lets us run our technology every day and sometimes in odd and difficult situations. We're learning a lot."

He paused, then he leaned forward again and spoke in a lower, more serious voice. He seemed embarrassed. "Actually, I never wanted to be a policeman, but I have to admit that it is satisfying in some respects."

Amanda raised her eyebrows, waiting.

"These people we're investigating are terrible," he said. "They're not desperate people committing desperate crimes to feed their children. They're stealing and loving it—living large. They've got friends as crooked as themselves and they have nothing but contempt for the general public."

"Really?" she said.

"Totally. They think they're like aristocrats and the rest of us are stupid and weak."

Amanda started to reply, but the waitress came back with wine and bread. Greg and Amanda had a general toast and a nibble.

Amanda said, "It seems to me this is all kind of dangerous. Aren't you worried about that?"

Greg said, "No, we're quite a ways back from the front lines."

When Amanda raised her eyebrows he added, "We're investigating stock market manipulation, not drug cartels."

"Okay." Amanda had another concern. "Why is the corpse restrained?" When he didn't answer she prodded. "The corpse is really dead, right?"

"Well," he drew the word out then paused again before explaining. "Cells in a body are really individuals in many respects. Some of the earliest creatures in evolution were actually just colonies of cells. Human cells have their own life cycles. Many of the cells in our corpse are still alive."

"Isn't that like cancer? Where the cells go their own way."

"Not really. Cancer is more like a revolt or a revolution. The cells actively attack the body. Here it's more like the central government has failed but the grocery stores are still open and the garbage is still being picked up."

He stopped and Amanda prodded again about the restraints.

Greg nodded and continued. "So muscles contract, that's what they do. We don't always know what sets them off but they do contract now and then and we don't want them damaging things."

Amanda could understand that.

A salad appeared and was, like the wine and bread, excellent. Amanda changed the subject again. "Do you think there's any chance your life may get more normal when this initial phase is over? Get some public recognition?" She smiled, second glass of wine in hand. "Enjoy your success?"

Those prospects seemed to please Greg. He took a moment to organize a response. "Once the government gets their own medical people involved and up to speed, Kenny and I will refocus on developing artificial nerves."

"So definitely not staying with the government?"

"No. This business with the post-animate interrogation was a lucky discovery. It has made us enough capital to go ahead with nerve development and productization, but we really didn't go into medicine so we could be cops.

"Why did you go into medicine?" She ventured a mischievous smile. "To help people or to make a whole lot of money?"

"To help people," he replied, less than amused. "Certainly when I was a kid—sort of a generalized desire to do good works. But later, when I got older and as I started to understand more about the body . . . maybe when I began to realize how much I didn't understand about the body . . . then I saw that it was what I wanted to do with my life.

"Our artificial nerve work is not a cure for cancer or even the common cold, but there are neurological problems and they are serious problems for the people who have them. We should be able to really improve the situation for a lot of those people."

Two waitresses appeared with the entrees. Both of the young women were lovely, and both went virtually ignored by Greg whose attention remained on Amanda. She had ordered a concoction of crab and shrimp. She was impressed to see that Greg had found something that actually looked like meat and potatoes. The crab shrimp was a disappointment; too rich, but she should have known.

Between bites she asked, "So you will stay dedicated to the business, no family or personal plans?"

"Not in the short term. The work we've done here, with the corpses, has given us a good understanding of how our nerves work in the body, but productization is a whole other deal. We'll have to do market research, we have to design new nerves—ones that doctors need and that we can manufacture. We have to have a factory, employees, patents . . ." Greg stopped, seemingly overwhelmed by the scope of the future undertaking.

So a no on family and personal life, thought Amanda. She was a little hurt and a little curious that he hadn't asked her any similar questions—questions about her personal life. Then she realized that he had her personnel records. *Divorced, no dependents, moved here for the job. Emergency contact a friend in New York.* He knew perfectly well how on her own and vulnerable she was. Her stomach twisted, and she quickly looked away from him.

Still, she had caught herself occasionally mugging for his attentive gaze and later, when they were back on the ward, she kissed him—several times.

CHAPTER 4

The Osiris team consisted of Zeke Keele and Jessica Miller. They shared an office in the Manhattan South Federal Court building. They did not have a window, but they did have a door. More often than not, the door stayed closed.

Zeke and Jessica worked for Freddy Logan, Chief Federal Prosecutor for Manhattan South. In addition to court room prosecutions, Zeke and Jessie did the basic analysis work on the highly secret Osiris material, pulling out facts and connections and linking them into the division's existing intelligence database. Access to this enhanced database was limited to Jessica, Zeke, and Freddy.

Freddy chose when to make cases and who to make them against. He was also their only connection to the Osiris source. He brought the new material to them and he communicated follow-up questions back upstream somewhere.

The block the little team occupied on the organization chart had a vague label and the actual term "Osiris" was seldom spoken aloud outside of their office. The various working groups within Manhattan South were isolated from each other by Chinese walls. Attorneys from different groups didn't talk "business" and it was considered rude, if not unethical, to inquire into other people's cases.

"Has Freddy said anything about Sarah Russell?" asked Zeke.

Jessica looked up from her computer with a faint air of irritation. Zeke sometimes thought of her, stick thin and wearing large, heavily framed black glasses, as an elegant praying mantis. "Freddy hasn't said anything to me."

Zeke got up and put on his suit coat. "I'm going to go ask him."

"There's some crisis or another. I'm pretty sure he's in the war room." This was a mild warning. The Chinese walls of the office dictated that if it wasn't your crisis you weren't really supposed to be in the war room.

But the rule was not ironclad and Zeke decided to risk it. He needed to know the status of any possible deal with Sarah Russell.

FREDDY LOGAN WAS short and trim. His hair was bright red, his movements were crisp and sure, and he spoke with authority. When Zeke came into the war room Freddie motioned to him, granting him a percentage of his attention as he, Freddy, moved around the room, giving instructions and asking questions of the half-dozen investigators working the electronic smart-wall screens like artists touching up a mural.

"Did you get a chance to look at the Sarah Russell interview notes?" asked Zeke.

"Yes." Freddy worked his way toward a far wall that had drawn several laser pointers and a heated discussion.

"And?" asked Zeke, trying to keep pace.

"I don't want a deal."

That surprised Zeke. "There's a lot of new information in there."

"Pillow talk and rumors," said Freddy. "Mrs. Russell was a decorative woman . . . probably ran some errands."

Zeke didn't think so. He came close enough to speak under his breath. "We know from the Osiris source that she attended meetings with Wickliffe and Sam Arnold. This stuff about Stophonix is certainly interesting."

Freddy shrugged. "We don't need her. No deal."

"If she's so unimportant, why execute her?" It was a fair question but his voice was a little loud.

Freddy bristled at the tone. He turned to Zeke. "Loot the market on the way up, loot the Treasury on the way down. We're going to put a stop to that kind of thinking."

Then he added, "Sarah Russell conspired to destroy the life savings of thousands of people, tens of thousands of people, and she did it so she could get a bigger house at the beach."

When Zeke still didn't respond, Freddy continued. The whole room was listening now. "How do you have a society of laws in a society without ethics?" he asked. Everybody in the room knew it was Freddy's favorite question and Freddy answered it himself. "Rigorous enforcement."

CHAPTER 5

Greg and Kenny's operation, Glimmer Development, was located in the massive new veterans' research hospital at Goshen, New York. Glimmer occupied a small, secure ward behind double doors off a second floor hallway. The reception room, the room where Amanda had sat for months, was now occupied by a temp from the Administrative Services pool.

At the rear of the room, to the right of the receptionist's desk, was a single door to the ward and a deserted nurse's station. That door was heavy and secured with a touch lock. Beyond the nurse's station a gloomy hallway stretched back into the building. It ran past an empty waiting room, a set of his and hers restrooms, the staff lounge and canteen, supply closets and a half-dozen patient rooms. At the end of the hall was a set of locked, windowless double doors that opened into a laboratory.

Behind those double doors, inside the laboratory, Kenny, Greg, and Amanda were playing a lab version of baseball. The ball was soft plastic, re-purposed ammo of a spring-powered semi-automatic bazooka. The billy club sized bats were souvenirs, remnants of the mountain of memorabilia from a celebratory trip to the World Series that Greg and Kenny had made when they got their first really big check from the government.

Greg pitched and Kenny caught. Amanda had played sports in high school and was comfortable with a bat. She waggled her shoulders and hips menacingly.

"Come on Gregory, we need an out," said Kenny. "Don't go easy just because she's your girlfriend."

Greg frowned and pitched the ball.

It floated in nicely and Amanda popped it up a bit to Greg's right. With a good stretch and a little jump he one-handed it.

"Damn," said Amanda. She thought playing with the geeky toys was cute and probably the sort of thing brainy people did, but despite the twenty-four-seven nature of their operation, it felt a lot like goofing off and it made her uncomfortable. This seemed like a good place to stop, so she laid down the bat. "I'm about finished scrubbing down the lab," she said. "If I start now, I can probably get that done before I have to go cover for the temp so she can go to lunch."

Kenny grinned. "Wickliffe needs a sponge bath."

The image she had been nurturing of the more or less dead man was vague and conceptual. He was the focus of their enterprise, a not particularly nice man who had come to a bad end. She had built a neat little fence around that image in her mind, and when she looked at Wickliffe, she crossed her eyes a bit to blur her vision.

But Kenny's suggestion, that she give him a bath, caused her to glance suddenly across the lab at the dead old man, naked under a sheet, steadily getting greener and smelling worse. Her stomach lurched, she felt nauseous and her knees threatened to give way. But she kept her composure as best she could and smiled sweetly at Kenny. "As tempting as that offer is . . ." She went to finish cleaning the refrigerator that held blood for the heart-lung machines.

"We'll need her help if we wind up with two of them," Kenny said, speaking to Greg. "I hope she's not as squeamish with the 'Reliably Stunning'."

Amanda turned, a question on her face. "Reliably Stunning" rang a bell.

HOSPITAL STAFF CLEANED most of the ward but they were not allowed into the laboratory. Amanda wiped out the refrigerator and returned the blood supply to it. Wickliffe was leaving soon and a new "guest" was expected, so the refrigerator was temporarily crowded with blood for both corpses. For Mr. Wickliffe they had used type O red cells and AB plasma, the universal supplies, but the new blood was AB negative and had been ordered specifically. Greg and Kenny hoped that the more precise blood supply and a more sophisticated heart-lung machine would keep the corpse fresher and allow longer and more productive questioning.

She finished with the refrigerator, put away the cleaning supplies and washed her hands. "I'm going up to relieve the temp and then I'll go for lunch myself," she said. "Can I bring you guys something?"

"Not today. They've got chili dogs. We're going up ourselves later."

She rolled her eyes. "The way you guys eat, I can't believe you're real doctors."

"That's the Hypocritic Oath," Greg said with a straight face. "Do as I say, not as I do."

Amanda shook her head in mock exasperation and went through the double doors. She stopped by her room to pick up her purse and went out to the reception room and took over the desk. The mail clerk came by to drop off what looked like a software module and pick up a couple of outgoing equipment orders.

Glimmer did almost everything via snail mail. Greg said they worried about surveillance. Snail mail was certainly vulnerable but not as much, Greg and Kenny thought, as phone lines or the Internet. Amanda wasn't sure if they were afraid of surveillance by the people they were working for or the people they were working against. She chatted for a moment with the young man pushing the cart. When he left, she discreetly got into a desk drawer and checked to see when she had sent the order for the blood. Almost a month ago. Kenny and Greg had known a lot about the next "guest" for quite a while.

The admin came back from her lunch break and as she settled behind the desk she said, "Mrs. Olson turned you in."

Amanda, caught off guard, struggled for something to say. Mrs. Olson was head of administrative services.

"There are no secrets in admin services," said the temp with a coy smile. "Mrs. Olson sent word up the chain of command that she had inquired about your new duties here and that you had declined to respond."

The young woman paused, then, quite solemnly, continued, "Word came back down the chain of command that Mrs. Olson should mind her own damn business, thank you, and that Amanda Wilson was no longer any of her damn business."

Amanda laughed. The temp looked at her inquiringly, smiling again, seeking some clue perhaps as to what Amanda and the two young doctors were up to back there behind the big locked door.

Amanda chose not to take the opportunity to enlighten her and instead made the long slog through the hallways up to the cafeteria. She stopped at the convenience store and nick-knackery and picked up a paperback, one of the few things she'd forgotten to bring from her apartment. In the cafeteria she bought a chicken sandwich to go. When she got back to the ward, she sat alone in the canteen and ate. Before she returned to the laboratory, she heard Kenny and Greg go by on their way to the cafeteria.

The lab was sixty feet wide and twenty feet deep. The double doors were in the middle of a long side and, when Amanda came through the door, the equipment and bed for the new corpse were set up on her right. Wickliffe occupied the center of the room. The other end, the end to Amanda's left, had become the storage corner. There were a couple of computers, several large screen video displays, empty boxes, assorted packing materials, small tables and a smattering of office chairs. Amanda walked back into the equipment corner to the little work space she had cleared. She regularly worked there with transcripts. Her job was to edit the transcripts into something readable. In the end the documents would be titled Osiris and sent to the government contact.

As part of "coming up to speed" she had done a superficial reading of the transcripts of the Wickliffe interrogations.

The transcripts were created as digital files by speech recognition software. Amanda entered the phrase "Reliably Stunning"—the phrase Kenny had used—as a search string in her reader. She found the phrase and loaded the interrogation session.

Once she had the session open she remembered that it contained a bit of what she had thought doggerel. That had gotten her attention. She thought the corpse was trying to sing. There were even some sounds like laughter in its voice. It had frightened her, and she'd asked Greg about it. He'd explained that it was a parody song about some congressional scandal, that Wickliffe sang it because he thought it was funny. He explained that the humor was attached to the memory—like emotion.

Amanda went to the corpse and started an interrogation session. She retraced the questioning in the transcript.

Wickliffe described a bar in Manhattan and a party there. She understood the corpse's speech much better now than she had when she'd heard it during her "coming up to speed" period. A musical satire group, "Rocks On And Off", had been performing at the bar and Wickliffe repeated some lyrics. The first time through it had been all she could do to pick out words from the guttural speech. It was only the cadence that had made her realize it was music.

"They came down to Washington and filled the till." Then a chorus. Then, "Said they had a problem with a little bill."

"Yeah, they filled the till, yeah, we killed the bill, then we all kept still."

Now she heard it clearly and could make out the structure of the song.

"They got caught and well that's sure sad. But now we're all on TV looking really mad. Shaking our fingers 'cause they were so bad."

As her fluency with the speech improved, the pace of the interrogation shifted away from questioning and toward conversational. Wickliffe began to relate events, picking up the narrative. He was in the bar, singing along.

There was a woman there, the Reliably Stunning Sarah Russell. She was mouthing the words, too, and smiling. I asked her if she knew the song being parodied.

"Da Doo Ron Ron," she had replied over the din. "The Crystals."

"You're way too young for classic rock," I said.

She didn't answer, instead she got quiet, drew into herself. She did that often enough that people had noticed. The conventional wisdom was that she was thinking and the standard advice was get ready to duck. But I didn't think so. There was something pensive about her. It didn't seem to me that she was thinking—more like she was remembering.

And then she was back, smiling like before. "Nobody's too young for classic rock," she said.

"Or too old," I thought in my own pensive moment.

CHAPTER 6

Andy Crane was disappointed with his failed efforts to stop the pending execution of Sarah Russell.

But now he was talking to a new client about plea bargaining an uncharged crime. Andy particularly did not like plea bargaining uncharged crimes. It was tricky business for a defense attorney. The attorney did not have an obligation to report the crime, but he did have an obligation to keep the client from doing it again. If the client disclosed the crime to the attorney and then decided to back out before the authorities were contacted, the defense attorney and the client were left in an awkward situation. Andy had tried to explain the dilemma to Leonard Andrianopoulos but Mr. Andrianopoulos, a relative of a friend of Andy's law firm partner, had come to Andy's office as a new client with his mind made up. "I want to plea bargain an uncharged crime," he said.

Andrianopoulos was a big man, as tall as Andy, but where Andy was long and lanky Andrianopoulos was built like a lineman on a high school football team. Andy guessed Andrianopoulos was somewhere in his early thirties. He worked in a federal office that dealt with drug approvals and he seemed not just nervous but scared.

"I can tell you that the local feds are not particularly generous right now," Andy said, thinking again of his failed efforts to prevent the pending execution of Sarah Russell.

But Andrianopoulos persisted. He shrugged and his remaining defensiveness fell away. "I've been divulging internal information that is being traded on in the stock market. I want to make a deal."

Andy sat back and let Andrianopoulos tell his story.

"I work in federal drug approval," he began. "I'm not a researcher or investigator, I work with process regulation, essentially I dot i's and cross t's. But I hear things and I see things. It's not a locked-down office."

Andrianopoulos paused, his composure coming back a little, and he looked around Andy's office—a family picture: wife, two adolescent children and a dog. The rest was warm and comfortable but impersonal.

"About five years ago," Andrianopoulos said, "a guy offered me cash for whatever I heard, and I've been working for him ever since. It hasn't made me rich, but it's kept me in nice cars and a comfortable social life."

He stopped and scanned the office again, seeming to settle finally on the window with its view of the building across the street.

"Why now?" asked Andy.

Andrianopoulos thought for a moment and then said, "They're getting everybody now. It's not a bust here or a bust there; it's like they're spraying weed killer for crooks. Sooner or later they're going to get to me, and I expect it would be better for my customer if I were dead when that happened."

That was not totally unreasonable. "What do you want?" Andy asked. "Immunity, reduced sentence . . ."

"I want a new identity," he said.

That *was* unreasonable. It was the sort of thing Andy had been worried about. "What have you got to offer?" he asked. "Your customer. A list of the information you sold him?"

Andrianopoulos had thought it through. "Knowing what I sold will point to who's trading on the information." When that didn't seem to impress Andy, Andrianopoulos continued. "And sometimes my customer gave me information to try to verify."

"So you think there are other people in your office also selling information?"

"Yes."

"Okay," said Andy, "but they may know all or parts of this already. The feds may not need your information. Also, they are probably not going to view you sympathetically. If you had an invalid mother or a sick child they might be more understanding, but it sounds like you spent the money on sheet metal and fine wine."

Andrianopoulos paused again. "Do you remember Stophonix?"

"I've heard of it," said Andy, interested.

"It's an anti-stroke medication, a preventative. It would have been a great breakthrough and meant huge savings in medical costs, but two years ago the government published a study showing serious long term side effects."

"Okay," said Andy.

"The study was being released on a Friday morning. I called my customer and a little while after that, the study was held. The stock continued rising until the study was finally released the following Monday afternoon."

Now Andy paused a moment. "You think the study results were held so that insiders could get out of the stock before it collapsed."

"More or less."

"That's interesting, but . . ."

Andrianopoulos interrupted, "That's interesting but what's really interesting is who authorized the hold. Before the study was to be originally released, I notified the office we report to. That's the process."

"So you think the order to hold the study came from that office?"

"That office had to know that it was being held," said Andrianopoulos.

Andy was not sure of the significance.

"That office," said Andrianopoulos, "is a cabinet secretary's office. William Campbell—friend and mega donation bundler for the President."

CHAPTER 7

In the hallway, coming back from the bathroom, Kenny heard Amanda and Greg in the canteen, talking softly and laughing. He stopped for a moment, trying to hear what they were saying. When he realized they were talking about where to eventually build the Glimmer artificial nerve factory complex he shook his head and moved on down the corridor.

At the end of the hallway he went through the double doors and back into the lab. Wickliffe had not been responsive, so Kenny moved a small cart with a cranial nerve programmer up beside the bed.

The programmer was a bulked-up numerical keypad with a thin data cable coming from it. It communicated with the artificial nerves and served primarily to set their output power levels. During normal implant on a living human being, the surgeon would use the programmer to get the nerve operating at the default power levels. When the patient regained consciousness the surgeon would use the programmer to tune the nerve for best performance. It was anticipated that with a living human being the settings would be valid for years. But the corpses were always changing and needed tuning more and more as they decayed.

On the end of the programmer cable there was what looked like a bug, a plastic case about twice the size of a guitar pick with four little feet. Kenny touched the feet against a small sponge containing adhesive and then stuck it onto Wickliffe's head, just above his right ear.

The corpse moved.

Kenny jerked his hand away. The movement was stronger than anything he had seen a corpse do before—and it repeated. Kenny had never known that to happen either. He flipped the sheet off the right leg and saw the muscles contracting rhythmically—driving short, powerful movements against the ankle restraint. Small dots of blood had started to appear where the skin had been rubbed raw. The blood from the heart-lung machine, loaded with blood thinners, would not clot normally. In addition, the effectiveness of the dead man's immune system, if he had one at all, was an open question.

Kenny got hold of the leg and yelled for help. He could not stop the movements but if he anticipated the timing and threw his weight against it, he could lessen the impact of the corpse's flesh against the restraint. He yelled again and then realized he didn't know if the lab doors were open or closed. If they were closed, Greg and Amanda couldn't hear him calling. The corpse's leg continued to drive powerfully toward the restraints. Kenny was weighing his options when Greg and Amanda's running footsteps echoed down the hall.

"This leg is spasming," Kenny shouted as they came through the doors.

They hurried to the bedside. "Can you hold it?" asked Greg.

"Not much longer," said Kenny. "We need a syringe of muscle relaxer."

Greg moved beside Kenny. "Okay," he said when he got his hands firmly on the leg, "you get the syringe."

"You sure?" asked Kenny.

"Yeah, I got him."

When Kenny moved away Amanda stepped to where he had been and got her own hands on the spasming leg. She and Greg together managed to absorb the force of the kicks and limit the impact with the restraints.

Kenny came back with a syringe and injected the muscle relaxers.

Greg and Amanda held fast, and the spasms diminished in force and then tapered to a stop. Greg nodded to Amanda, and they both let go.

"We're going to have to stop this immediately if it happens again," said Kenny. "The blood is full of thinners and if he ever starts to bleed, he'll never stop."

"I'm pretty sure we can get a vibration detector at the mall," Greg said. "Off-the-shelf home security systems usually have those. We can probably get one and just put it in the bed."

"What's it trying to do?" Amanda was trying to clean up the blood around the ankle restraint.

"It's just the muscle contracting," Kenny had another syringe. "It's like a reflex. We don't know what sets it off." He injected more muscle relaxer into the corpse's leg. "When this takes effect, we can take the ankle restraint off and try to treat that abraded skin."

"Why did you say 'it'?" asked Greg.

Amanda turned toward him, perplexed. "Why did I say what?"

"You referred to the corpse as 'it', you didn't say 'he' or 'Wickliffe'."

Amanda shrugged, not sure she could explain—but she hadn't called it "it" by accident.

CHAPTER 8

The door to Freddy Logan's office was ajar but Zeke Keele, prepared to wait patiently, knocked and then turned and looked out over the bay of cubes to the windows beyond. He was a big man and hanging out in the hall could be awkward, but Freddy heard the knock and invited him in.

"Close the door," Freddy said. His laptop was open and his red head was down, focused on the machine. He motioned vaguely toward the two chairs in front of his desk.

Jessica Miller already sat in the chair farthest from the door. Zeke glanced at his wrist watch.

"I was a few minutes early," she explained.

"Have you had a chance to look over Leonard Andrianopoulos's proffer?" asked Freddy.

Zeke and Jessica exchanged a nod. Andrianopoulos and his lawyer, Zeke's friend Andy Crane, had negotiated a plea bargain deal that promised Andrianopoulos a new identity. Andrianopoulos and Crane had put together a proffer of the information Andrianopoulos would testify to, and Freddy had given copies to Jessica and Zeke.

"Good." Freddy closed his laptop and looked up with raised eyebrows. "What did you think of the business of a cabinet secretary holding up a research report?"

"It didn't actually say the cabinet secretary held the report," said Zeke.

"No," said Freddy, disappointed, "but he may have."

And Zeke did actually agree with that. Secretary William Campbell was somewhat qualified for the position he held but his main qualification, and the bedrock of his deep and personal friendship with the president, was Campbell's ability to raise and deliver large bundles of campaign cash. The idea of some quid pro quo bureaucratic malfeasance did not come as a shock. But you couldn't prove that by what Andrianopoulos had proffered.

"It sure looks like the other side of the deal we heard about in Osiris," Jessica said. "Andrianopoulos's call got things started and then, on the back end, Wickliffe learned from Sarah Russell that the report had been put on hold."

Freddy nodded. His office was spartan. The only items on display, aside from official tokens of achievement, were pictures of his dog, a King Charles Cavalier. The brown and white Cavi and Freddy's all-consuming affection for it were the only aspects of Freddy's life or personality that anyone in the office ever joked about—and then only behind his back.

"I want you to make this a priority," said Freddy. "With both ends of the string we should be able to work our way to the middle."

Zeke had doubts. "Do you think they'll let us handle this? Anything this close to the White House is usually up a couple of pay grades."

Freddy cocked his head and a bit of a smirk lit his face. "I deleted the incident from the copy of the proffer that went out generally. The three of us are the only ones who've seen it."

That gave Zeke additional pause. The three of them were also the only ones who had access to, or who were even aware of, the Osiris source.

Freddy made a little circular motion with his index finger. "There are ears everywhere here," he said. "I don't think there are actual crooks—well there probably are a couple of actual crooks—but there are a lot of people with political loyalties and obligations. Word would get around pretty quickly."

The phone rang but Freddy ignored it, focusing instead on Zeke—whose face had apparently betrayed his doubts. "What do you think, Zeke?" Freddy asked. "Concerns?"

"Well," said Zeke reluctantly, "I do have concerns. We've got this Osiris source that is so good and so conveniently relevant to whatever we're investigating." He gave a faint shrug of his shoulders and looked at Jessica for possible support. No such luck. "And now," he went on, "we're investigating a cabinet secretary's office. We're going to investigate the office of a man appointed directly by the president of the United States . . . and it's all a secret mission."

Freddy waited but Zeke had had his say. Instead Jessica broke the silence.

"I've thought about it too." She took off her black glasses and fully revealed her surprisingly nice eyes. "But we often have vaguely sourced material. It's the nature of investigations. The better the source, the better it's protected." She used the glasses as a pointer to nothing in particular.

Zeke knew that to be true. He also knew that responsibility for the propriety of the source fell primarily on the people who ran it.

"And if there is corruption that close to the president," Jessica continued, "you can bet the president wants to know about it."

Freddy followed along, nodding in agreement. He looked at Zeke for concurrence. Zeke tried for an expression of grudging acknowledgment, reluctant acceptance of the truth of what Jessica had said.

And, of course, it was true . . . as long as the president truly did want to know if there was corruption in his administration, and assuming that the people doing the investigations didn't have their own agenda.

CHAPTER 9

Mr. Wickliffe had been rolled off the ward in a closed white tube with "Hyperbaric Oxygen Therapy" stenciled on its side, and Sarah Russell arrived in what looked to Amanda, to be the same contrivance. It was a little after normal office hours and the pool receptionist had left for the day. Amanda was behind the reception desk when two young men in doctor's scrubs, the same two who had wheeled Mr. Wickliffe off, wheeled Mrs. Russell in.

"We have a patient transfer to Glimmer Development," said the shorter of the two men.

Amanda still had some uneasy feelings about the propriety of Glimmer Development in general, and the scripted formality of this transfer felt positively illegal. Greg had instructed her to ring for him when the transfer came. She rang now, and he appeared promptly.

"We have a patient transfer to Glimmer Development," said the shorter of the two men again, this time holding out a tablet.

"Terrific." Greg took the tablet and signed the displayed form with a touch. "Anything else?"

"No, sir." The men left quickly. Greg nodded to Amanda to lock the front door, and he rang Kenny.

Kenny came up and the three of them rolled the tube back to the laboratory. They had cleaned up Wickliffe's space, but the bed and equipment still occupied the center section of the room. They wheeled the tube to the right where a second bed and new equipment had been installed for the late Sarah Russell.

When they got her out of the tube and onto the bed, Greg handed Amanda a heavy pair of scissors. "Get her clothes off." When Amanda hesitated he said, "She won't be needing them."

Amanda started to cut. *It is a hospital*, she thought, *and they are doctors*.

Sarah Russell wore no makeup and her hair had simply been combed back out of her eyes, but her plain, unadorned face was lovely.

The flesh was still warm, not 98.6 but well above room temperature. As Amanda understood it, the body had been airlifted from the prison where the execution had occurred.

With the clothes out of the way, Amanda shaved Mrs. Russell's head. Kenny installed a TPN port for intravenous feeding and repositioned the body. He used a small, black wireless remote to adjust the bed. Then he put Mrs. Russell's left arm up and over her head in an arc and turned her face to the right. She looked like she was sleeping.

Greg moved the heart-lung machine closer to the bed, rolled in a couple of trays of instruments, and got the IV started.

Amanda's job was monitoring the heart-lung machine once it was attached and running. To that end, she got enough thawed blood from the refrigeration unit to fill the machine's various reservoirs. She got seated and reviewed the three readouts she would be watching. If any of those readouts got out of bounds or if a warning beep sounded, she would alert Kenny and Greg.

Kenny made a four-inch incision between the ribs on Mrs. Russell's left side and deftly attached the tubes from the heart-lung machine into her circulatory system. When the tubes were secure and free of air bubbles, Amanda started the flow of warm, oxygenated blood into the body. She thought she saw an immediate result, subtle movements of the body on the bed, slight changes in the color of Mrs. Russell's skin. Her lips seemed fuller and her cheeks flushed with the fresh blood flowing through.

Kenny brought up a tray with the artificial cranial nerves. He got a small handheld electric saw running. The high-pitched wine of its motor dropped dramatically when he started cutting into Mrs. Russell's head.

CHAPTER 10

Andy Crane, in his trademark pearl gray suit, had been handed a plastic key when he checked through security into the federal courthouse. In a sixth floor elevator lobby he passed the key in front of a mirrored wall and a panel popped open. He slipped through, into the interior passages of the federal court house. The hidden door closed automatically behind him. Once inside it took him a moment to adjust to the narrow, relatively featureless corridors. Small precise signs identified doors and pointed directions at hallway intersections.

His occasional visits into the interior of a court house always made him think of it as the last of the powerful temples that had ruled the ancient world, the temple of justice with its secret passages and robed priests.

He passed a jury lined up in two rows like kindergartners, poised to make a dramatic entrance into a jury box. They scrunched cheerfully against the walls to let him pass.

The invitation to visit Judge Hardt in his chambers was not unprecedented, but it was a little unusual. The judge did maintain personal relationships with many of the attorneys who appeared before him, but Andy didn't think he was quite due for one of his periodic visits. Hardt's clerk exchanged pleasantries with Andy and sent him back to the judge's office.

The judge, working at his desktop computer, motioned for Andy to sit down. Andy took the plusher of the two chairs in front of the desk. The judge's office walls were lined with his collection of expensively bound law books. They were obsolete in the computer age, a statement in favor of former times.

"How are things at your house, Andy?" the judge asked without looking up.

"Good," said Andy. "Olivia, our fourteen-year-old, is turning into a real soccer player. We're having a good season."

The judge finished at the keyboard and turned to Andy, smiling. "I particularly like soccer. Two of our grandchildren play. A good reason to leave work and spend an afternoon outside in the fall." The judge had silver hair and gold-rimmed glasses and he wore a crisp white shirt with a starkly blue tie. He opened a desk drawer, took out a magazine and handed it to Andy. "I saw this on the way in this morning."

Andy nodded. He had a copy of his own. The magazine, a pop culture weekly, had Sarah Russell on its cover. Inside, ten pages were devoted to her story. The magazine portrayed her essentially as a sympathetic victim of American greed and her own good looks. Andy thought the article seriously slanted in Mrs. Russell's favor but it did not purport to be serious journalism. The focus was on her upscale life in the city before her arrest; on her beautiful children, her beautiful home, her beautiful self. That they contrasted with her childhood—a mother with serious substance abuse issues and a father she never knew.

There were also lovely pictures of her beach house from a home and garden article. There was coverage of her charity work and pictures from elite fund raising events with powerful leaders and celebrities. Pictures taken with her husband in happier times described him only as the owner of a popular restaurant. Andy had sensed deep and bitter divisions between them but the article contained no hint of that.

But as sad as all that was, as charming and likable as Mrs. Russell could be, and as admirable and impressive as her climb from difficult circumstances had been, she had been convicted of serious crimes that were glossed over or dismissed in the text. There were no pictures of the people whose lives she'd wrecked making the pile of money she'd spent so elegantly.

Andy laid the magazine back down. It was something of an awkward moment for him and the judge given their individual complicity in her death—the judge ordering it, Andy unable to prevent it.

"I wish it had turned out differently," said Andy.

"I wish she hadn't done it," said the judge. Then he asked, "She did offer to talk, didn't she?"

"She did, but they weren't particularly interested."

"Why not, do you think?"

Andy took a moment to phrase his response. "She absolutely didn't want to talk at the beginning and I expect they doubted her sincerity." He thought of Leonard Andrianopoulos. "They also seem to be getting a lot of cooperation from other sources."

"So you think you were treated fairly in the Russell case?"

"Yes." Andy felt he'd been invited to the Judge's chambers to answer that question. "We didn't have much time between the conviction and the execution but I don't think there's anything we could realistically have done with more time.

That seemed to satisfy the judge. "Good." He changed the subject, though not back to Olivia's soccer season. "You have any idea where all of this is going to end?"

Andy cocked his head and his eyebrows crept higher.

The judge explained. "The Watergate investigations were pretty much about getting Nixon and Agnew. The Savings and Loan . . . you know the Savings and Loan Scandal?"

"I've read about it."

"They did some prosecutions," said the judge, "enough to take the edge off the public clamor. Then they shut it down."

"My understanding is that there was more to it than that," said Andy with all the good nature he could muster. The judge could be touchy about his conspiracy theories.

"Depends on who you read I guess. The point is, both political parties cut off funding to any candidate who tried to run on it in the next campaign."

Andy hadn't read that. "Why? To keep the media coverage down?"

The judge nodded and smiled with a trace of cynicism. "They didn't want to shake public confidence in the banking system."

Andy laughed.

"But this is different," said the judge. "There doesn't seem to be an obvious target, the public's not demanding anything. Confidence in the financial system is going up, not down."

Andy thought again about Andrianopoulos. "This is more like broad-leaf weed killer. I had a guy, Leonard Andrianopoulos, walk in out of the blue and offer to give himself up. He said it's like the feds have got a weed spray for crooks and they're just working their way through the financial institutions and the government."

The judge thought a moment. "Somebody should get them a budget increase," he said finally.

CHAPTER
11

The new woman, though she was spooky, held something of a fascination for Amanda and she was disappointed not to be involved in actually interrogating the corpse. Instead, she was relegated to editing the transcripts into readable Osiris documents and fact checking those against the stacks of testimony and paperwork that had accompanied the body.

Amanda could hear the interrogation going on sporadically at the other end of the lab. She was surprised at how clearly she could hear the differences in the sounds Mrs. Russell made compared to those of Wickliffe. But Amanda could not make out the words, and she focused instead on the transcripts of the sessions that kept piling up in the inbox of the little office she had carved out of the clutter.

The tale of corruption the late Sarah Russell was telling appalled Amanda. The callous manipulation of markets and investors and the contempt for the law and the public were stunning. Sarah recounted instances of blackmail, drug use, sex for favors, rumored mob connections, and payoffs to government insiders. Through her husband Frank, who owned and ran a very high profile New York restaurant, there were criminal connections to entertainers, politicians, and people in broadcast journalism.

But the heartlessness of the prosecution disturbed Amanda as well.

They had seized every scrap of Sarah Russell's personal property, everything she had the faintest claim on. In the end Sarah had offered to talk, to make a deal so she could live and her children would at least know their mother. But the government had not been interested, and Amanda remembered that she herself had placed the order more than a month earlier for a supply of blood in Mrs. Russell's exact type. How fair was that trial?

At eleven thirty Amanda closed up her little shop for lunch. Mrs. Russell wasn't talking, the body had its own cycles, and they had to adapt. Kenny and Greg worked in shifts. Kenny had his laptop open, typing away.

Amanda paused a moment to look at the dead woman. She seemed fresh and pretty, like she had just gotten out of the shower and wrapped her hair in a towel, just as Amanda often did.

"I think I'm going to go eat in the cafeteria," Amanda said. "Can I bring you something?"

Kenny looked up from his computer. "No, thanks. Greg and I are going up together when he wakes up."

She left the lab and headed to the front to cover the desk while the receptionist went to lunch. Amanda still handled quite a bit of the office paperwork and she spent the half hour catching up on the receptionist's desktop. The time went quickly, interrupted only by the regular visit of the mail cart. When the receptionist came back, Amanda left for the cafeteria.

The Goshen Research Hospital was a massive facility. She seldom recognized people she passed in the halls, so she was surprised when she turned a corner and realized that she had seen the man behind her before. He was older, late thirties or even early forties, wearing a sweater—some sort of computer guy she thought. Greg had said they were probably being watched, and she wondered.

It was a good quarter of a mile hike through the halls, with an elevator ride, to the main cafeteria. As she got closer to the cafeteria it felt like coming out of the suburbs and into downtown. A tiny bank, a cleaner's, and the little convenience store sat in an alcove. A display at the entrance of the convenience store had a magazine with a picture of Sarah Russell on the cover.

Startled, Amanda stared for an instant, then glanced around and saw that the man in the sweater had paused at the cash machine outside the bank. She hesitated. *Screw him,* she thought, and bought the magazine. With it under her arm she crossed the hall to the cafeteria, dutifully filled a plate at the salad bar and sat alone, picking at the salad and reading.

The text helped flesh out Sarah Russell's life in the penthouses and skyline suites of the big city. Amanda was particularly interested in the details of Sarah's relationship with her husband, but the article mentioned him only as the manager of the family restaurant.

The writers did not dwell on Mrs. Russell's legal problems. They hinted, in fact, that she had stumbled into her life of crime because it pervaded the office where she worked and that she had been thrown to the wolves when things went wrong because she was high profile and pretty.

But it was the pictures that moved Amanda—the stunning radiance of Mrs. Russell's smile, the children she so obviously adored, the ease she seemed to have with fame and power. The images of the vibrant young woman who was now the tricked up corpse back in the lab was more than Amanda could bear. Tears welled in her eyes and she worried that she could not control her face. She scooped up the magazine and left.

Back in the ward she nodded to the temp and then headed straight for the lab. She had the magazine open to Mrs. Russell's story when she popped through the double doors, eager to share it with Greg.

But neither of the doctors were in the lab. Disappointed, Amanda started toward her nook.

Vague sounds came from the corpse and Amanda turned quickly. She knew the corpse was entering an active phase, so she crossed to it. Amanda thought a moment, picked up the microphone and hefted it tentatively in her hand. Then, curious about the husband, she began asking questions. She went over what she knew from working with the transcripts. Mrs.

Russell answered her questions about the illegal trades and drug deals that she and her husband had participated in. Amanda was surprised by how easily she could follow the speech of the dead woman. Finally, she decided to try to get at Sarah Russell's feelings about her husband.

"What do you think of your husband?" Amanda asked.

The corpse paused before uttering a string of slurred words that Amanda understood as: "How could such a jerk, father such lovely children?" A low grumble followed that Amanda recognized as a chuckle. She laughed too.

"That was my sister's opinion," said the dead woman.

Even with the monotone of the voice box Amanda could discern the rhythm of Sarah's voice and some inflection. As it had with Wickliffe, the interrogation slipped into conversation. Mrs. Russell began to relate events.

It was late afternoon, and it was raining. I was sorting through the little antique writing desk in the second floor library. A lot of interesting stuff ends up in that desk—odd bits of old jewelry, expensive collectibles, memorabilia—stuff like that. I'm not sure why.

My sister Martha and I were in the library with the four kids, her two and my twins. Her girls were a little older. They sat at a table, big girls coloring. Martha was on the floor, wrangling the twins. Those three were having hilarious times.

The second floor library has always been my favorite room. It has a high ceiling and tall windows that overlook a quiet, tree-lined street. I was looking for a miniature portrait and I was a little desperate. I wasn't sure where I'd tucked it away. I had to report to jail in two days and I wasn't coming home right away. Maybe never.

The small painting had belonged to Grandma. She claimed the woman was my great-great-great-great grandmother. There was a family resemblance, to Martha and me and to our mother. My mother was always after Grandma to let her have the painting. My mother was not remotely sentimental.

So when Grandma passed away and the miniature came to me I had it appraised. I don't know if the woman in the portrait is Martha's and my great-great-great-great-grandmother but I do know that she is

Peggy Eaton and that she was a central figure in the Petticoat Scandal during Andrew Jackson's administration. I also know that the miniature is an original oil and worth upwards of a hundred thousand dollars.

I was relieved when I finally found it. It had got shuffled to the back of a drawer. It was in a little velvet envelope and I slipped it into my pocket.

I would have liked to give it directly to Martha but technically it is against the rules, and Martha is not good at breaking the rules. She cannot tell a convincing lie and it's agony for her to keep an important secret. I'm not complaining. I'm glad she's that way. I did what I could when we were kids to make her that way, but it complicates life sometimes.

Instead, I'll give it to Andy Crane. Andy will take it if I tell him it's a family heirloom and I want Martha and the girls to have it. He doesn't have to know how much it's worth.

CHAPTER
12

The second quarter charity fund raising drive at the federal courthouse had exceeded goals by twelve percent and the chairmen who had overseen collections in the various departments attended a debriefing and celebration in a third floor conference room. Freddy Logan had attended and, on the way out, after the meeting, he snagged an extra celebratory cup of ice cream with a little wooden spoon. He'd just taken a bite on his way back to his office when he ran into Zeke Keele. Zeke drew him aside.

"What's on your mind?" Freddy asked.

"I'm wondering about Andrianopoulos," Zeke said. "We've pretty well finished up what we can do without his testimony. Any idea how soon we'll be getting him?"

Freddy thought a minute, scooping up another bite of ice cream. "I'm thinking maybe a week. I still need two signatures."

Zeke would have preferred sooner. He and Jessica were eager to talk to Andrianopoulos about the information he'd promised in his proffer, particularly the call he claimed he made to the office of Secretary William Campbell about the Stophonix report. But Zeke did not carp at bureaucracy. Andrianopoulos getting a new identity took a lot of paper work. "Any chance of a surveillance report?"

"Yes." Freddy brightened. He had one team of federal agents

trailing Leonard Andrianopoulos and another doing constant and detailed monitoring of everything electronic Andrianopoulos owned or touched. Freddy didn't think Andrianopoulos was telling them all he knew. "I'll get that to you this afternoon," Freddy paused and then added, "We did sniff out another contact. We have seen Andrianopoulos meeting once in a while with Sam Arnold."

Zeke straightened up. "Sam Arnold. I know the name."

"He's an old fixer, financial stuff," Freddy said. "A known associate of the late Norbert Wickliffe."

Zeke remembered then. Sam Arnold had introduced Sarah Russell to Wickliffe.

CHAPTER 13

"I don't think our government pals are going to go to the mat for a couple of," Kenny made air quotes, "independent contractors." When Greg didn't respond Kenny elaborated, "Independent contractors making pots of money."

Amanda had nodded off over her transcripts. She sat up when she picked up on the conversation. Greg and Kenny stood near the body of Sarah Russell. They seemed unaware of Amanda's presence.

"We're not doing anything illegal." Greg spoke in a calm and soothing voice.

Amanda stood up.

Startled, both men turned toward her.

"Our Ms. Wilson," Kenny said, "lurking about."

"I'm sorry," Amanda said crisply, irritated at the gratuitous dig. "I dozed off."

There was an awkward moment. Finally, Greg said to Amanda, "Sarah Russell made a second offer to testimony."

"And the feds said no?"

"Yes," said Greg, "and Kenny thinks—"

"And Kenny thinks," said Kenny, "that we are culpable in her execution."

"All we are doing," said Greg, "is using our techniques . . ."

"All we're doing is making boatloads of money and getting the business ready to launch on its own," said Kenny. "That's all we're doing and that's all you care about."

Greg shook his head. "You know that's not true."

Kenny stood over the corpse. "They executed Sarah because of us."

"They executed her because she was guilty." The volume of Greg's voice crept up.

Heedless, Amanda joined in. "We ordered the blood in her type specifically a month before she got here. They planned to kill her all along."

Greg glared at her. "That doesn't mean anything," he said. "The prosecutors knew they had the evidence, and they knew they were going to get the verdict. They knew she was guilty." The sharpness of the exchange seemed to startle all three of them and for a moment they were quiet—everybody calming down. Greg said, "The point I'm trying to make is that we don't have half the facts, not remotely half the facts but you two are ready to pounce, to accuse the government of something rotten or sneaky."

"That's not fair," Amanda said defensively, though she grudgingly conceded the point.

Kenny did not. "She offered to make a deal and talk, and they executed her anyway. Then they sent us the corpse because they knew we could get the information."

"She wasn't going to tell them the truth," Greg said. "You heard what she just said. She wasn't going to implicate her husband Frank."

Kenny moved away, still angry.

"What do you mean she wasn't going to give up the husband?" asked Amanda.

"Just now, when we were interrogating, she told us she was protecting him in return for his giving custody of the children to her sister," said Greg.

"But that didn't happen," said Amanda. "I saw in the magazine article. The husband still has custody."

"Well she thought he was going to, but the execution was scheduled so soon that it didn't happen before she died."

"And he double crossed her!" said Amanda.

That night Amanda thought about the execution of Sarah Russell and the treachery of Sarah's husband. Amanda also thought about her own position as, technically, a double dipping federal employee making her own little pot of money. She wrote a brief note and a check for a thousand dollars. The next morning she discreetly went through the case files and found the home address of Andy Crane, the lawyer who had defended Sarah Russell.

At noon Amanda went up front to relieve the receptionist for lunch. The receptionist headed for the cafeteria and Amanda pulled out the second drawer on the right-hand side of the desk. Toward the back she had an eclectic collection of personal cards—birthday, get well, happy anniversary, etc. She selected a nice looking birthday card, inserted the note and check and then carefully addressed the card to Olivia Crane, Andy Crane's daughter, and, as an afterthought, decorated it with a couple of doodled in little hearts. When she finished, she put a stamp on it and dropped it in the outgoing mailbox.

CHAPTER 14

There was a lot of interest in Amanda Wilson's letter when it arrived at Andy Crane's house. Olivia Crane, to whom the letter was addressed, was fourteen and her mother, Elizabeth Crane, who first saw the letter, didn't think the girlish doodling on the envelope was in step with the sort of thing her daughter's friends were likely to do.

Olivia, when summoned, did not recognize the handwriting or the art work and opened the letter with a great deal of curiosity. She and her mother discovered then that the letter, and the check that accompanied it, were meant for Mr. Crane. While it was unusual, unusual things often occurred in relation to Mr. Crane's career. They called him, outlined the situation, and sent the envelope and its contents to his office by courier.

The letter was really a long, hand-written note. It was signed by an Amanda Wilson and postmarked at the Veteran's Research Hospital in Goshen, New York. It began "Dear Mr. Crane" and then continued. "I was a close follower of Sarah Russell's trial and I know she trusted you."

Andy at first thought the letter was from a marginally deranged person, a sort of fan. A woman sitting in upstate New York and soaking up the media coverage of Sarah Russell, imagining a personal relationship.

But Andy took the next few sentences more seriously. "I also know," Ms. Wilson wrote, "that Sarah Russell had an arrangement with her husband. She would give the government no information about his criminal activities and in return he would give custody of the children to Sarah's sister Martha." The letter went on to list four companies in whose stock Mr. Russell had allegedly traded illegally.

Crane checked on his computer. The stock of each of the four companies had had a volatile trading stretch in the last few years. Insider trading was, in fact, suspected in the case of one of them. But Andy could find no implication of Frank Russell, Sarah Russell's husband, in any trading irregularity and no mention of him in any illegal or unethical behavior of any kind. Still, there were the names of the four companies and Andy had always felt that Sarah Russell was protecting somebody.

And there were the last lines of the letter. Amanda Wilson wrote, "I am not totally sure of my own position in this situation. Please accept the enclosed check as a retainer against your services."

In the end, Andy decided that the letter was worth investigation. He set researchers on the four named companies and on Frank Russell. He put the private investigators he did business with, Morgan and McGown, on the trail of Amanda Wilson—"be extremely discreet"—he'd instructed. Next he called Martha Simonson, Sarah Russell's sister, and set up, in vague language, an appointment with her. Finally he endorsed the check for deposit and called in an admin.

CHAPTER 15

Amanda sat up on the edge of the bed and pulled on a sweatshirt. "What are you doing?"

She turned her head and smiled. "I'm getting some clothes on," she said. "Then I'm going back to my own room to get properly dressed. Then I'm going to try to get some work done."

Greg lay in bed, covered with blankets up to his chest. "I don't want to work."

"If we don't do anything, Kenny will know and he will feel cheated," she said. "He'll think we were goofing off while he took care of his sick mother."

"He *will* wonder what we've been up to," Greg said and swung out of bed, looking for clothes.

Amanda was a little disappointed that he was so amenable to common sense.

Kenny had gone to take care of his sick mother. He had a sister and a brother, but they were both caught up in short-term emergencies of their own and so it fell to Kenny to cover a few days while Mother recovered from pneumonia.

He'd been gone for two days, and Greg and Amanda had embraced the freedom and privacy of having the ward to themselves. They had managed basic maintenance on the corpse of Sarah Russell and had coped with the cleaning people, but interrogation and the production of Osiris documents had stopped.

When Amanda, properly dressed, got back to her little desk in the clutter of the equipment corner she felt a pang of dread when she saw the transcripts still waiting in her in-box. Their break from the job had been nice, but it made her realize what a drag the twenty-four seven work schedule had become.

Greg came in and started working with the corpse. Soon she heard the sounds of interrogation, though she couldn't make out the words. She got started again on editing the transcripts. Ten minutes in, she came across the transcript of the informal little session she had done—Sarah and Martha talking in the library.

She didn't understand how that session had gotten into the transcripts. She asked Greg to come over. When he did she showed him the transcript.

"I did this interview," she said. "I wanted to know how Sarah felt about her husband. How did it get in here?"

"It's automatic," he said. "The equipment automatically records all the speech during an interrogation and sends it through the voice recognition software."

"I don't think this should go in," she said. "It's just her talking about her husband with her sister."

"I haven't read it."

Amanda took a moment to organize her explanation. "There's this business about a miniature portrait," she said. "Sarah wanted to leave something to her children. She wasn't trying to cheat the government, she was trying to get around her husband. She planned to ask Andy Crane to take it for her and hold it for the sister."

"Andy Crane. Her lawyer?"

She nodded.

"Wouldn't that be illegal, maybe unethical?" he asked.

"But Andy Crane didn't know how valuable it is. He thought it was just some semi-precious family heirloom."

"But it's still illegal," he said.

"But isn't that like entrapment?"

He looked down his nose at her. "Did you study law?"

"No," she said brightly. "But I watch television."

Greg got up and headed back toward the corpse. "But you don't want to put it in Osiris," he said.

"No."

"You feel like you were eavesdropping and now you're ratting her out."

"Well," Amanda said. "Yeah."

CHAPTER 16

Andy had gotten to know Martha Simonson during the trial of her sister Sarah Russell. Martha had been in court on key days and she had often accompanied Sarah to meetings with the defense team.

Martha was a middle school teacher and her husband was a professor of meteorology. They lived with their two young children in a pleasant house on Long Island. Andy made the drive up the island to meet with her. It was not a school day and Martha was home with the children. He got there mid-morning and after checking on the children Martha served him coffee at the kitchen table.

"How are you?" he asked when they were settled.

"I'm okay," she said. "The kids are having a hard time with it. Sarah's girls are too little to understand but mine are a little older and they know something bad happened to Aunt Sarah. It's difficult."

"I'm sure. Do you have Sarah's twins a lot?"

"Yes," she replied. "Frank is awfully busy, and he knows I'm always glad to have them."

Andy took a small package from his jacket pocket. "I don't know if this will help or hurt."

Martha opened the package and her face lit up. "It's great-great-very-great grandmother," she said. It was an antique miniature painting of a dark-haired woman. Martha looked up and asked, "Do you know the story?"

"Yes," said Andy. "Sarah told me."

"There is a real resemblance," Martha said, examining the painting again. "Particularly to my mother and to Sarah."

"And to you."

Martha Simonson was a softer, less dramatic version of her sister. In all aspects of Martha's appearance and demeanor, those chosen consciously and those not, she avoided the sharp edge and aggressiveness of her older sister. But Martha was every bit as pretty as Sarah and if she didn't stop traffic it was because she chose not to.

After a moment Martha tilted her head and asked, "Why did she give it to you?"

"I don't think she thought that you'd be comfortable lying about it. Technically it should have been turned over to the government with her other property."

"She always said I was a terrible liar." Then Martha asked, "So this is illegal?"

"Not very, I think," said Andy, "since it's a family keepsake. She told me she wanted to keep it away from her husband Frank, not the government."

The sound of a crash came from upstairs along with competing shouts of "Mom". Andy and Martha exchanged an amused glance, and she got up and headed off like the cavalry.

Andy had a typed list of the companies Amanda Wilson said Frank Russell had traded illegally. He opened his brief case, took it out and laid it on the table.

Upstairs, the drama played out. He heard some movement of furniture, charges and counter charges exchanged in childhood soprano and resolved in the calm but stern adult voice of a mother.

When Martha got back, she refreshed the coffee and said, with the wisdom of a middle school teacher, "Children are not born civilized."

He smiled and had a sip of coffee. "This is a little awkward. I'd rather not tell you exactly what I'm thinking or why I'm thinking it."

Martha was a little startled.

Andy continued, "I think Sarah and her husband had agreed that he would give custody of the children to you."

"You mean if something happened to him?"

"No," said Andy. "Right away."

"Really?" She thought a moment. "You know," she said finally, "Sarah used to say things once in a while. Stuff like 'when you have custody you can . . .' but I never took her seriously."

"Did she kid around a lot?" Andy asked. He didn't remember that she did.

"No," said Martha with a faint smile. "It was just with me. She lied to me all the time."

He knit his eyebrows and gave her a quizzical look. She nodded and explained, "I was about ten when Mom disappeared."

"Your mother disappeared?"

"Yes. Sarah said it was with a man with a whole lot of money."

Andy had not known that.

"What Sarah actually said," explained Martha, "was a man with a whole lot of money and better drugs."

"How sad," said Andy.

"Yes," said Martha with a little shrug. "But after that Sarah pretty much raised me. Grandma loved us and she did her best but she was too old and Mom had worn her out."

"When I got to be a teenager I realized Sarah lied to me about where money and stuff came from and about some of her friends. We fought about it until I got old enough to understand that she was protecting me. That she wasn't proud of some things and she didn't want me to know."

She stopped then, and they sat in silence until Andy asked, "And you've been content since, never knowing the truth?"

"Sarah never did a mean thing to me," Martha said, "and she gave me my life."

CHAPTER
17

Dr. Kenny Conklin stood in front of a rotating greeting card display rack. He balanced a large brownie on a paper plate and tried to gracefully stay out of the way of other people moving around the coffee shop, their own hands filled with hot liquids and sticky treats. He had his eye covertly on two seats that were reasonably isolated and against the wall, but he didn't want to sit down until he got his mocha.

His mother was better. She was home from the hospital and seeming more like her old self, sleeping less and keeping food down. He expected his sister to arrive in the afternoon to take her turn as caregiver and he would be free to go back to work at Glimmer.

The mocha came up and Kenny took it to one of the two seats he had been eyeing. He slid the sturdy wooden chair as far back from the table as he could to minimize the space between it and the wall. He had a privacy shield for the screen of his laptop but it didn't do any good if the peeper got directly behind him.

The computer was small and powerful. From his pocket he took a thumb-sized flash drive and slotted it into the laptop.

The flash drive held an elegant suite of off-the-shelf software and space to run it. The software components included a sophisticated and devious browser that presented itself randomly as one or another of the most popular commercial products, a military grade encryption capability, and background processes that teased and parsed out internet address headers and wove an algorithmically created tale of plausible imaginary calls and plausible imaginary responses.

Kenny typed a URL into the browser and connected to a site on the deep web. Satisfied with the precautions he'd taken, he was not concerned with safety. The array of dangerous and illegal activities on the deep web was matched by the horde of half-wits and mental defectives lurching about in the space. If anyone, or anything, picked up his access he would be a needle in a haystack, a haystack of pins.

And then, if their tools were very good, they could at best place his anonymous presence at random locations on the southwest side of Chicago.

He spent forty-five minutes visiting sites he had bookmarked, adding a couple more, and jotting down notes in a paper notebook. He had all he thought he needed, and he was reassured that the organization he had settled on was a foundation. Loose ends all tied up, he shut down his laptop. Ready to return to Glimmer at Goshen.

CHAPTER 18

"I think that's a coworker," said Little Blue Dog.

The images of Leonard Andrianopoulos on the video screen were sharp and clear and he seemed to be up to no good. Zeke Keele watched from the surveillance van with Little Blue Dog and Big Blue Dog. Andrianopoulos was in the produce section of a supermarket, subtly trying to get the attention of a woman two carts away.

"Blue Dog Three," said Big Blue Dog, "can you get a shot of that woman for facial recognition?"

"The woman in the green dress by the apples?"

"Yes."

Zeke had been unsure how he felt about the cost of the surveillance van. It was certainly comfortable, but surveillance was a tedious business. Some luxury did not seem an unreasonable thing. The van was relatively new—although it seemed to Zeke that on the few other occasions he had been involved in surveillance those vans had also been relatively new.

The leather was maybe too much, that and the plush swivel chairs and the carpet. The video screens were large and sharp but they were certainly necessary for the job. People doing surveillance needed to eat and restrooms were required.

On the other hand, a tax payer's watchdog group might find it excessive—all those little extras could sure bump up the sticker price.

Zeke rode along with the surveillance team because he felt that he had done all he could without an in depth interview of Andrianopoulos. Zeke's boss, Freddy Logan, said there were still some sign-offs to get things clear for the new identity and relocation deal that Andrianopoulos and his lawyer, Zeke's friend Andy Crane, had cut. Zeke thought that probably true, but he also knew that Freddy didn't entirely believe Andrianopoulos. Freddy thought Andrianopoulos knew more than he was telling them, that he was only giving up enough to get his new identity deal.

And now Leonard Andrianopoulos seemed to be proving out Freddy's suspicions. The woman in the green dress finally noticed him and Andrianopoulos worked his way over to her.

"There's a crackdown at the office," he said softly.

The woman gave him a questioning look.

"They're watching the office," he said. "Bugs everywhere."

"How do you know?" she asked.

The catch was a shot of adrenaline for the surveillance team. Chatter picked up between the van and the resources on the ground in the store. The two chase vehicles were re-positioned.

"Believe me, I know," said Leonard Andrianopoulos. "Keep your head down."

Too late for that, thought Zeke with an ironic little smile.

CHAPTER 19

"Could we talk a bit?" asked Martha. She meant just the two of them.

Frank Russell, husband of the late Sarah Russell, understood that and looked a little puzzled. After a pause, he said to his new friend Erica, "Sweetheart could you get the twins settled in the car?"

Erica was young and pretty and seemed quite nice. She smiled pleasantly and hustled the little girls around the table to give Aunt Martha a hug. Then, smiling again and working in a "glad to have met you" she set out for the car with her charges and their gear.

The luncheonette had large windows along the wall next to the street and Martha could see her car and Frank's. They had met midway to hand off the twins.

Martha mentally reviewed the plan that Andy Crane had laid out and screwed up her courage. "Sarah told me," she said, "that you and she were working on an arrangement for me to get custody of the twins after she was gone." Andy had argued that, technically, that was almost true.

No sign in Frank's face betrayed surprise or discomfort. He did turn his gaze out the window to where he could see Erica moving the children toward the car.

When he turned back to Martha, he said, "We had discussed it but nothing definite. Things moved so quickly toward the end."

Frank smiled and his eyes seemed warm and sincere. Martha remembered what her sister Sarah used to say. "Frank is only really interested in people he can screw—one way or another."

Martha dug in her purse and pulled out a small piece of paper. It was a copy she had made in her own handwriting of the list Andy had given her. "I did find this list of stocks that Sarah said you were interested in." She handed Frank the piece of paper.

Andy had told her that there were questions about some of Frank's stock transactions. Martha thought she saw a flicker of anger cross Frank's face when he read the list, but the anger vanished almost before it became visible.

"I don't recall these," he said as he put the list in his pocket, "but I will have my accountant take a look at them. I'm sure they're important if Sarah thought they were."

Outside, Erica had the little girls in their car seats and was putting their backpacks in the car.

"We're going to lose the restaurant," he said, maybe changing the subject, maybe not. She didn't know. She struggled to match his look of dejection.

Sarah had hated the restaurant. It was, she said, a great stage and playpen for Frank and an ongoing financial disaster for the family.

The waitress brought the check and topped off coffee.

Frank picked up the check and Martha said thank you. Then he brought the discussion back to the twins. "Sarah and I had decided that it was best if you took the girls," he said. "We thought they would be better off in a stable family environment."

He paused and sipped his coffee. "I thought it would be better if we waited awhile, until the family got a little less famous."

She understood that, but she asked, "Why didn't you tell me?"

"I should have," he said.

He looked out the window, toward the car. "I just thought it would be easier to wait until we were ready to do it. Things seem to be settling down for the girls and I thought we should just let that happen for a while."

Martha knew that Andy would have wanted her to press for some commitment as to when the custody transfer would occur but she decided to quit while she was ahead. She walked out to the cars with Frank and got another good-bye hug from the little girls. Then she headed back out Long Island.

CHAPTER
20

It was almost dark and the white caps of waves breaking down on the beach caught the moonlight. I had left the party for a minute and stepped out onto the long screened-in porch that ran along the south side of the house. I was trying to remember where I had stashed my cigarettes when I smelled burning tobacco.

There were chairs and a few small round tables along the wall with the house and at one of them, in the shadows, I could see three women and the tips of at least two glowing cigarettes.

"The bad girls," I said.

There was polite laughter.

Then I asked, "Have you got an extra?"

A little more polite laughter. "Join us?"

I found a chair and a cigarette and lighter appeared.

Two of the women worked for a national financial news channel. One was a morning cohost, and the other was a bond market expert. The third woman was a New York reporter for one of the major networks.

"Great party," said the bond market expert.

"Great house," said the New York reporter.

I nodded. "We love being near the water," I said. "We're lucky to have it."

The others agreed. We all sat in silence for a moment, listening to the waves. Then the bond market expert asked dramatically, "What did you do with the edamame?"

"Yes," said the cohost. "It's fabulous."

I smiled. As I was relating the recipe the phone in my ear went off. I spoke a moment into the air and then rang off. "Hostessing," I said. "But . . ." and then I finished reciting the recipe.

"Amanda," Greg said, interrupting the interrogation. "Have you got a minute?"

Amanda pulled herself away from Sarah Russell's recitation.

"Do you have a copy of the last report we sent to Osiris?"

Amanda realized that Kenny had come back. Surprised, she said, "Hello. Welcome back."

Kenny shrugged. "Yeah," he said.

"How's your mother?" Amanda asked.

"She's pretty well over it," he said, brightening a little. "My sister is there for another week. The doctors say Mom should be okay on her own then."

"Oh, good," Amanda said, genuinely pleased. "You are lucky to have that."

Kenny didn't seem to understand what she meant.

"You and your brother and sister," she said. "Your mom. It's wonderful that you work together for her."

"It's just family," said Kenny.

Amanda started to say, "When my mother died," but she didn't. Instead she said, "It's nice you work together and do that."

"Yes," he conceded finally, "it is."

Greg asked again for the transcript. "Kenny wants to get back up to speed."

"Sure." Amanda started for her little office in the corner.

Kenny moved over next to the corpse and checked the vital signs.

"Amanda, why don't you also get the last follow-up request we got," said Greg.

She thought it brusque, and figured he was uneasy about Kenny being back. It occurred to her that they were an odd little group—where simple civility could be something of a reach.

She got the documents and went back over to the corpse where Kenny still fiddled with instruments. She handed him the documents.

"Thanks," he said. "How's she doing?"

Greg answered, "We're still getting good results with interrogation but we've got the nerves tuned pretty high. Awfully high for this soon."

"And look at this." Amanda pulled back the sheet and exposed Sarah Russell below the waist. Her once elegant, fashion model legs had been replaced with the bulging, sharply defined muscles of an Olympic sprinter.

Kenny winced. "Just the opposite of what we'd hoped for with our younger, fresher corpse and the better targeted blood supply."

Greg nodded. "The autonomous cell growth is much more vigorous than anything we saw with Wickliffe."

They stood quietly for a moment. Then Greg brightened a little and said, "Amanda has been doing some interesting things with language. She's having really productive interrogation sessions."

"What does she do?" asked Kenny.

"She just seems to have an ear for it," said Greg. "She gets it to flow."

"The pace is like we're really talking," said Amanda. "I even have to throw in the occasional 'really' or 'oh' to keep them moving."

"You're kidding," said Kenny with an odd little grimace.

"No," said Greg. "She does it."

"Come see," said Amanda as she moved back to the microphone.

Kenny checked the vitals again. "Have you had to shock her yet?"

"No," said Amanda quickly, remembering the pitiful moans of Mr. Wickliffe. Then she started questioning Sarah Russell, letting the interrogation settle into a natural pace.

I went back inside and rejoined the party. It was a good looking crowd, though not movie stars and even a little too old for the bold and beautiful denizens of a Fortune 500 headquarters. But they were extremely well dressed and very well preserved. The thing that always struck me was how at ease they were with each other. It wasn't that everybody knew everybody, though everybody certainly knew somebody, but more a sense of belonging. They were comfortable with each other and comfortable with themselves.

The call had been about finding Frank. Someone wanted to talk to him and it wasn't good to get anybody wondering too much about where he was. I crossed several rooms, exchanging smiles and greetings but not stopping to chat. Then I slipped into a hallway like I was heading for a bathroom.

The house had been built by a US Senator in the 1920s and it had a secret room. Frank and I had had its walls lined to prevent external eavesdropping, and the room was swept regularly for anything irregular, electronic or otherwise.

There were several ways to get to it but you had to know where it was or be guided. I worked my way along, checking that I was not being followed, until I came to a panel in a little used hallway. I triggered a concealed latch and stepped into the hidden room.

Inside Frank was talking to William Campbell. Campbell was a major fundraiser for the president-elect and was being mentioned as a possible cabinet appointee in the new administration.

"Frank," I said, "there are couple of people needing your advice. They're on the verge of a search party."

Frank nodded. "I think we're okay here," he said to Campbell.

"Yes," said Campbell. "I think we've covered everything we wanted to talk about."

Frank left and I said, "We'll give him a few minutes and then I'll take you back."

"Sure," said Campbell.

"What do you think of the edamame?" I asked.

"Etta May?"

I laughed. "Edamame," I said. "We'll get you some when we get back. It's getting very good reviews."

Amanda stopped the interview session. "We've got Frank Russell in a secret conference with William Campbell."

"Future Cabinet Secretary William Campbell," said Greg.

"Yup."

"William Campbell from whose office the order to hold the Stophonix report probably came!"

"Yupper."

None of the three noticed the late Sarah Russell's hands. She was methodically ticking off her fingers with her thumbs . . . both hands . . . in unison.

CHAPTER
21

"Isn't Andy Crane a friend of yours?" asked Jessica.

It was morning and Zeke was eating a doughnut. He finished chewing and swallowed before he answered. "Yes, I've known him since we were kids."

"Well, he made the papers." She held up her copy of the new Osiris material.

Zeke didn't know how material from the Osiris source arrived in the Manhattan South offices of the Federal District Attorney, but it arrived on his desk by the hand of Freddy Logan. When Freddy had dropped off the new installment half an hour earlier he reminded Zeke and Jessica, as usual, that only the two of them were authorized to look at it.

"What page are you on?" asked Zeke.

"Sixteen," said Jessica. "It says that Crane took a hundred-thousand-dollar miniature antique portrait from Sarah Russell to hold for her kids until they were older."

Zeke finished his doughnut, wiped his fingers, picked up the document and found the page Jessica was talking about. He read a few minutes and said, "So she tricked him into taking it."

"She didn't tell him the whole truth."

They read in silence awhile and then Zeke slowly shook his head.

"What I don't understand is why either one of them would ever tell anybody. If word got out, Mrs. Russell's kids sure wouldn't be getting the stuff. Crane could face disciplinary action."

"So?"

"So, if neither of them told anybody, how'd it get in here?" Zeke indicated the Osiris document.

Jessica thought a moment.

"One of them must have told somebody," she said. "Maybe they discussed it on a phone and it got picked up."

"I don't see why they would have done that."

"I don't either but everyone makes mistakes," she said. "If criminals didn't make mistakes, we'd never catch anybody."

Zeke read the section again. Andy Crane and Sarah Russell were smart people and neither of them was likely to comment on anything important on a telephone or over a computer network. Finally, though, he moved on and read the next section. And there he came across another surprise. He found material implicating Sarah's husband, Frank Russell, in several illegal stock transactions. It was the second reference in the Osiris material to wrongdoing by Frank Russell and a contrast to what Sarah had maintained in her testimony and what had appeared in the press—that Frank was not involved in anything illegal.

CHAPTER 22

It was Saturday morning, a little after ten, when Andy came out of the supermarket.

With three bags of groceries in his cart he headed across the parking lot toward his car. Two men wearing suits intercepted him. At first he thought they were Jehovah's Witnesses or something. They were not.

Except for the eyes they could probably have been anybody. Their suits and haircuts were okay. They were large, sturdy men, but they weren't giants. They didn't look like body builders, but their eyes locked on Andy's and never left them—they betrayed no emotion and they never seemed to blink.

"Andy Crane?" the larger of the two men asked.

"Yes."

The man did not extend a hand to shake. Instead he said, "We're friends of Frank Russell."

Andy nodded, a little surprised. He knew Frank Russell fairly well and had never known him to associate with what Andy thought were clearly professional men.

"I'm a friend of Frank's too," Andy said.

The larger man did smile faintly then. "Frank doesn't think so."

It was a sunny day with an early hint of autumn. There were a lot of people moving around the parking lot and there were surveillance cameras.

"Frank had a visit from his former sister-in-law, Martha Simonson," said the larger man.

Andy was a defense attorney. He had had encounters with more than his share of dangerous people. He knew these guys were not going to go all histrionic and shatter his knee caps—not here anyway.

"Mrs. Simonson made what Mr. Russell took to be threats."

Andy did not feel compelled to stare down the two men. No use trying to scare them. On the other hand, "professional" men would know that threatening a high profile attorney was serious business and to do it in such a public place . . .

"Mr. Russell thinks," the large man paused. "Mr. Russell's friends think that you are behind Mrs. Simonson's . . . aggressiveness."

"I don't control Mrs. Simonson," said Andy.

"You'd better."

The two men left and Andy found his car and put the groceries in the trunk. He parked the cart in a corral and when he opened the driver's side door to get into his car, he saw a manila envelope lying on the seat.

He moved the envelope to the passenger seat. He assumed there would be someone watching, someone noting his reaction. He did not open the envelope until he got home, sitting in his parked car, before going into the house.

The envelope contained pictures. Eight by ten glossies of his kids. The pictures had been taken at school. Son or daughter walking in the hall, chatting with friends. Pictures taken in classrooms, the gym, even one in a bathroom in front of a mirror. They were recent pictures, he recognized the clothes.

It was not fear that Andy felt. It didn't have an adrenaline component. There was no twist in his stomach or flood of energy to his limbs. Rather it was a great weight settling on him, pulling down on his arms and legs, making them heavy, filling his heart with dread.

CHAPTER 23

Amanda was surprised to learn that, apparently, there are worse things to eat than cafeteria chili dogs. Kenny had teased her into trying one and she liked it. Of course it was a chili dog in name only. You needed a knife and fork to eat it. That the "chili" was chili was at best debatable. But she thought the flavor could become a guilty pleasure and with all those beans it had to have some nutritional value.

Greg came into the break room and seemed a little surprised to find them having lunch together. He came over and kissed her on the top of her head.

"He made me do it," Amanda pointed at Kenny.

"I'm sure." Greg got a cup of coffee and sat down.

"Did you hear from our friends?" asked Kenny.

"Yes." Greg took a sip of his coffee. "They say we have no additional guests scheduled in the short term."

"So," said Amanda. "We finish up with Mrs. Russell and get some down time?"

"There's maintenance we need to do," said Kenny. "There will be another one sooner or later."

Amanda finished eating and put the remains and plastic cutlery back into the Styrofoam container the whole thing had come in. She found that once she stopped eating she wanted to get rid of the mess and the smell as soon as possible.

"What I'm thinking," said Greg, "is that we should request that they send us a doctor or two."

The suggestion was a bit of a surprise to Amanda. Nobody spoke for a moment. Finally Greg continued, "If we are having a little slow time we could spend some with them—training, transferring the technology."

Kenny sounded doubtful. "I thought we were going to do documentation and work on getting our patent applications ready, things like that, before we called them in."

"And those things are important," said Greg. "But the sooner our government pals get their own people in here, the sooner they'll take over."

Kenny shot an accusatory look at Amanda. "And we suddenly want out of here as soon as possible."

Greg took a deep breath. "I thought you wanted out, Kenny. You've been pretty clear that you're uncomfortable with the ethics of what we're doing."

Kenny was silent a moment. "That's a different issue. The ethics aren't going to change just because somebody else is running it."

Greg sighed. "Of course." He turned to Amanda and asked, "How is Sarah today?"

Caught off guard, Amanda needed a moment to organize her thoughts before responding. "We do okay for a while, five or ten minutes, but then she starts fading in and out."

"I expect you'll have to start using shock," Greg said.

Amanda remembered again the terrible cries that had come from Mr. Wickliffe.

"Kenny can help you," said Greg with a little edge in his voice. "It's up to you."

She knew it was true. If they were going to finish the questioning, the corpse of Sarah Russell would need stronger stimulation as it decayed.

"I can help you with it," Kenny said to Amanda. "If you want me to."

CHAPTER 24

I looked up from the document I was reading. "This is a mob guy," I said.

"He's a respected businessman," said Frank. We were in the second floor library. It was night and the drapes on the tall windows were drawn.

"He's a respected businessman who's a front for the mob."

"How do you know that?"

"You told me, Frank. Six months ago. You pointed him out at the restaurant and you said, 'that's George Thornton. He's a mob front guy'."

Frank took that in stride. "They only want three percent," he said. "It's a generous offer. We need the money."

"Sell them the whole damn thing . . . or give it to them. Then we won't need the money."

Frank got up and made himself a drink. He offered me another, but I shook my head no.

"You always do this," he said. "Every time we have to talk about the restaurant, you do your little rant about how it's killing us financially, about how we don't need it . . . we have to have this obligatory spat before we can start discussing the issue."

Sarah's voice began to slur and Amanda couldn't follow it. Then the corpse stopped speaking all together.

Kenny had re-tuned the nerves for her but she felt she needed to deliver the shocks herself. She waited about ten minutes, as Kenny had suggested.

The shocks were controlled by a dial. The knob was calibrated one to ten. It moved easily and Amanda had to be careful and precise when she moved it. She worked it slowly up to two and the corpse began to squirm. At just short of three Sarah Russell gave a little cry and Amanda shut it down.

The second time she snapped it sharply to three, counted one-thousand-one, one-thousand-two, and snapped it back to zero. There was a sharp yelp from the corpse but the words started flowing again.

Why can't you just make a normal, respectable sale? There are people who want it.

"There are," said Frank. "But they won't pay as much and they'll want a controlling interest. They'll want to run the restaurant."

"And you don't think Mr. Thornton and his friends are going to want control?"

Frank shrugged his shoulders.

"A regular buyer would probably want to keep you around as the face of the business."

"Yes," said Frank. "I'd be a damn maître d'."

I didn't laugh but I could have.

Frank shifted to charm. His eyes lit up, and he grinned. "We do have a plan," he said.

"A plan? You and the . . ."

"Me and the respected businessman, Mr. Thornton. We're redoing the private rooms."

"Our private rooms are as good as any in the city," I said.

"Yes," said Frank. "But they're going to be better. We really do have a plan and it could work out much to your and my advantage."

"I'm not going to sign it," I said.

"I can't make you sign it," said Frank. *I thought there was a clear insinuation that there were other people who could.*

"I told them it was a deal," he said. "I took the money and I've already spent half of it."

Not long thereafter I signed the document.

CHAPTER
25

Andy Crane and Zeke Keele sometimes met after work at Third and Long, a sports bar with dark wood, rich imitation leather, and too many TV screens to count. Andy and Zeke had known each other since childhood and they often met casually to catch up and drink some beer. Their conversations were only occasionally about work but when they were, the two men were circumspect, carefully skirting the issues raised by their being on different sides of the ball.

So that morning, when Andy called and more or less insisted they meet, Zeke didn't know what to expect.

He got to Third and Long during happy hour. The saloon was loud and crowded with groups of apparent coworkers, some in suits but more in business casual. They were clustered around tables and booths or gathered in little clumps along the bar itself. Zeke looked around. Relieved, he saw a long, thin arm in a pearl gray suit waving from a booth along the back wall. He edged through the crowd and slipped into the small booth. A pitcher of beer sat on the table beside a glass for him.

"Happy folks," said Zeke, indicating the crowd.

Andy nudged the pitcher toward him. "Get happy."

Zeke looked at the beer. "What is this?"

"IPA."

"A pitcher of IPA," he said over the din as he filled his glass. "This is a civilized country."

Andy refilled his own glass. "I have a problem."

Zeke nodded. He had expected something in that vein.

"I had a follow up meeting with Martha Simonson, Sarah Russell's sister," Andy said. "Martha told me she thought Sarah and Frank had an agreement and Martha would get custody of Sarah's children after Sarah's execution."

Zeke didn't expect Andy to tell him the truth, or at least not the whole truth. It didn't offend him. Dancing around the facts could sometimes be necessary when the two of them spoke about the law and cases.

Zeke also knew that there had been an agreement between Sarah Russell and her husband Frank—that Martha would get custody of the children after Sarah's death. He knew that from the Osiris source. It did not seem at all unlikely that Martha Simonson would have learned about the agreement from her sister.

"I suggested that Martha talk to Frank about it," said Andy. "Let him know that she knew about the arrangement and ask what he planned to do."

A waiter came, and they ordered some appetizers. "She did talk to Frank," Andy continued, "and last weekend I was stopped in the supermarket parking lot by two guys, two thugs. Expensive thugs. Well-dressed and well-mannered but serious men."

Zeke straightened up.

"They said that they were friends of Frank Russell. They said that Mr. Russell had had an unpleasant conversation with Martha Simonson and that Mr. Russell and his friends thought I was behind it. I said I couldn't control Mrs. Simonson, and they said I'd better."

Andy paused, took a drink. "When I got back to my car I found a manila envelope with pictures of my kids. Pictures taken at school."

"Jeez." Zeke raised his eyebrows. "Did you report it to the police?"

"No," said Andy. "I don't think there's much they can do. I can't prove anything."

"They could provide some protection."

"I have security," Andy said. "A private firm—Morgan and McGown. I work with them regularly. We've needed security in the past. They've got people following the kids to school and back. The whole family is being watched."

"Including you?"

"Yes."

"What's Elizabeth think?"

The appetizers came and the two men took a moment with them. When Andy seemed content to graze, Zeke repeated his question. "What about Elizabeth?"

"I haven't told her," Andy said.

"When are you going to tell her?" Zeke's voice was sharpening.

"I'm not."

"You've got to tell her, Andy. They're her kids too."

Andy frowned and looked away. Zeke regretted the tone of his remark. But he also thought that Frank Russell and his friends were having a pretty serious overreaction to being reminded about a custody arrangement. Zeke knew from Osiris that Frank Russell had been involved in several illegal trades with his wife Sarah and he wondered if perhaps Martha, or even Andy, had known about these trades and brought them to Frank's attention.

"There's nothing Elizabeth can do except worry," said Andy finally. "The police can't add much to our security and they will want to talk to Frank."

"So why are you telling me?"

"So that if anything happens to me somebody will know the score," Andy said. "Somebody who can do something about it."

"And other than that you're just going to keep your head down and hope it goes away. Just ignore the gangsters lurking around the edges."

Andy smiled perfunctorily. "I'm not going to do anything to piss off Frank Russell."

"What about Martha Simonson?"

"I didn't tell her about the threats. Frank told her that he would turn over custody when the family was 'a little less famous.' I suggested we give him some time, and she thought that was okay."

"So you and Mrs. Simonson won't do anything to upset Frank," said Zeke. "What if somebody else does?"

Andy straightened up slowly and looked at Zeke. Zeke could almost see him thinking.

"Are the feds interested in Frank?" asked Andy. "Are you guys going after him?"

Zeke returned Andy's gaze and shrugged. They both knew they couldn't talk about that.

CHAPTER 26

There were thirty folding chairs under the blue canopy. Kenny sat alone in the front row, the row nearest the open grave. The other mourners were leaving, drifting off in little groups toward their cars. It was a pleasant and sunlit day—vaguely cool with the first hints of the coming fall.

A minister came to Kenny, to give some comfort and perhaps prompt him toward the exit. The minister touched Kenny's shoulder and spoke a kind word. Kenny looked up with a face so twisted with grief and anger that the minister turned away as if stung.

The minister mumbled an apology and moved off.

Kenny's mother had died unexpectedly. She had seemed to be recovering from pneumonia when it all went to hell one night and she was dead by morning. There was an undiagnosed heart condition lurking under the pneumonia that had been discovered too late.

Kenny's sister wanted to sue but Kenny knew there was no suit. The medical team and the hospital had followed all the best practices. His mother's condition was a fluke and the only one to blame, Kenny knew, was he himself. He knew his mother, and he knew the science. If he'd been paying attention , been being a doctor, he would have seen it coming. At least he would have known that something was not as it should be, known that something else needed to be checked.

But Dr. Kenny Conklin hadn't been doctoring. He'd been distracted, his mind still in upstate New York, playing mad scientist with corpses. And he could see the result. With proper treatment his mother would have had a good ten more years of healthy, active life. Instead she was toes up in a coffin, waiting for somebody to start throwing dirt in the hole.

CHAPTER 27

The surveillance van sat in the dark on a narrow one-way street. Two doors down, a restaurant and all-night convenience store provided most of the light and all the activity in the neighborhood of otherwise closed businesses.

Leonard Andrianopoulos was having dinner in the restaurant with Sam Arnold, the friend of the late Norbert Wickliffe. They were finishing up and the surveillance resources were moving around, getting themselves outside without exposing the coverage.

Zeke Keele watched the surveillance screens in the van. Of the four screens, only one had video of the target. Blue Dog Three, standing near the bar, got a good shot of Andrianopoulos and Arnold making their way toward the door.

Multiple working groups in the Second District Federal building were interested in what Andrianopoulos would have to say when he was eventually pulled in, and Zeke's boss, Freddy Logan, was building a priority claim by having Zeke log time in the van.

One of the Blue Dog resources caught Andrianopoulos and Arnold on video coming out of the restaurant. They stood by the door for a moment and then headed up the street. Two men stepped out of the shadows in front of the convenience store and started shooting. Andrianopoulos and Arnold went down. Shouts came over the audio in the van and the video feeds briefly lost focus. The two shooters ran. There were shouts of "Halt" and "Federal Officers." Shooters from the Blue Team opened up.

Zeke realized, with an enormous and joyful rush of adrenaline, that one of the running men was headed toward the surveillance van. Zeke undid his seat belt and opened the door a couple of inches. He watched the video feed, calculated the moment and flung the door open and leapt at where he thought the man would be.

The man wasn't there. He had seen the door open and dodged to his left and cleared it without breaking stride. Zeke did hit the ground running but Big Blue Dog landed on his back and the two of them crashed to the concrete.

Another blue team member hurtled past the two downed men and ran on in pursuit of the gunmen.

Blue Team Leader held Zeke on the ground. "Easy counselor," he said. "You don't have authorization to get shot."

Another blue team member flashed by.

"Nobody's shooting," said Zeke.

Two bursts of machine gun fire raked the sidewalk from up the street. Bullets cracked around Zeke's head and knocked chips out of the concrete. Big Blue Dog pulled Zeke over the curb and tried to squeeze the two of them under the van. "This is not amateur hour," he said.

A barrage of single shots and the sound of more running feet came from across the street. *The guys from the chase car*, Zeke thought. Somebody screamed in pain. The machine gun started up again but quickly fell silent in another volley of pistol shots. Finally, somebody called, "We're clear."

Zeke got to his feet with difficulty.

"I'm sorry," said Big Blue Dog. "That had to hurt."

Zeke looked at the divots in the concrete and remembered the crack of the bullets. "It's all right. Thanks." He struggled to conceal his shaking hands.

Big Blue Dog got back in the van and Zeke moved down the street toward where Andrianopoulos and Arnold had been shot. Blue Dog

Three was there. "Looks like the guys with the automatic weapons were back-up," he said. "They opened up when we started firing."

"What about these guys?" Zeke waved a hand toward Andrianopoulos and Arnold.

"They're alive," said Blue Dog Three with a shrug. "For now."

Zeke got on his phone. Freddy answered on the second ring. "Zeke?"

"Yeah, Freddy. I'm with the surveillance van. Andrianopoulos's been shot. Sam Arnold, too. Couple of guys opened up on them when they came out of a restaurant."

"Are they alive?"

"Yes, but they're not conscious."

"Okay . . . are the city cops there yet?"

"No. Just happened." Zeke realized he had no accurate idea of how much time had passed.

"Okay. I'll get back to you."

Zeke put his phone away and turned to look at Andrianopoulos and Arnold. They lay where they had fallen. He couldn't see any blood. Blue Dog Three stood over them. Other members of the surveillance team had formed a perimeter against the slowly building crowd.

"Pretty straight forward ambush killing," said Zeke to Blue Dog Three.

Blue Dog Three nodded. "The machine gun up the street was a surprise."

Zeke acknowledged that.

"But it cost them," said Blue Dog Three. "They've got two guys dead and another two going to the hospital—solid candidates for the death penalty. Those guys might be interested in making a deal."

Big Blue Dog got out of the van and came down the sidewalk. "Just talked to your boss," he said to Zeke. "He wants it all zipped up. No press. Officially an inter-gang dispute. Bad guys killing bad guys."

A couple of black and white squad cars arrived, sirens wailing and lights flashing. Big Blue Dog went to meet the officers as they got out of the cars.

Zeke's phone rang. It was Freddy again. "There's an ambulance coming from the Veteran's Hospital for Andrianopoulos and Arnold. Get them on it and ride in it with them." He gave Zeke the name of the contact to turn them over to at Veteran's.

The crowd continued to grow slowly and more squad cars arrived, providing additional troops for the perimeter. Two ambulances came and started loading up casualties. A pair of EMTs with a gurney came to get Andrianopoulos and Arnold. Zeke waved them off. They came back with another guy from the ambulance brigade and Big Blue Dog.

"You're waiting for another ambulance for these guys?" the new ambulance guy said.

Zeke nodded.

"Insurance issue . . . not good at our hospital?"

Zeke shook his head.

The ambulance guy said, "I've got another ambulance on the way, two blocks from here, and my emergency room is the closest."

"Thanks, but we're good."

The ambulance guy looked at Big Blue Dog for support but only got a shrug. Then he said, "Hope they don't die on you. The paperwork's a bitch."

Zeke said thanks again, and the EMTs moved away.

When the ambulance from the Veteran's Hospital arrived, they got Andrianopoulos and Arnold onto the gurneys and into the vehicle. They put Zeke in a drop down seat against the front wall, just behind the cab.

He spent the ride trying to anticipate the jolts and lunges of the speeding ambulance and attempting to discern the condition of the two patients from the actions and conversation of the EMTs. He didn't have much luck with either.

CHAPTER
28

It was around 10:00 p.m. and the Glimmer facility at Goshen had more or less settled down for the night. The corpse of Sarah Russell was quiet. Amanda, Greg, and Kenny were working four hours on and eight off. Amanda was halfway through a four-hour shift.

Greg came into the lab, with a serious look on his face. "I got a call from the government. Kenny's asleep, but he's getting around. We've got kind of an emergency."

Amanda looked up from where she sat at her work station. "What's happened?"

"We might have a couple of unexpected 'guests'," he said.

"A couple?" She looked around the room reflexively. They still had the setup where Wickliffe had been. The heart and lung machine and the interrogation equipment were still in place. "When?"

"Tonight," he said. "Maybe tomorrow."

Kenny came in wearing rumpled sweats and stifling a yawn. "What's happening?"

Greg paused while Amanda joined him and Kenny at the foot of Sarah Russell's bed. Then he explained that the government contacts had called and there were two guys they thought to be key players now in the emergency room at Goshen. The two guys had been shot in Manhattan and brought to Goshen in an air ambulance.

"Are they alive or dead?" asked Amanda.

"For now they're alive," said Greg. "If they die they'll send them to us."

That seemed to wake Kenny up a little. "These are gunshot victims?"

Greg nodded.

"We've never done that," said Kenny.

"No," said Greg.

"Who shot them?" asked Amanda.

"It doesn't make sense to bring them out here," said Kenny. "What if they had died in the ambulance?"

Greg hesitated a moment, thinking. Then he said, "The government guy told me they were worried about protecting these men if they do live. They apparently have a lot to talk about. The government guys think they can protect them more easily out here if they live and if they don't . . ."

"It would sure improve efficiency." Kenny smirked. "If they want somebody interrogated just shoot them dead."

"I suppose," Greg said. "Maybe." He shrugged.

"Or better yet," added Kenny, "shoot them almost dead so you can keep them fresh."

"Do we have any idea of their condition now?" Amanda asked.

"No." Greg looked around the lab. "We may get them both or neither of them. We just have to get ready." He looked at Kenny. "If we get one and manage to get to interrogation we might find out who shot them."

Kenny didn't seem pleased, but he didn't have another comment.

Greg and Kenny started making a list of the equipment and supplies they would need. Amanda got busy cleaning up the equipment corner. They decided to store things in one of the empty patient rooms on the ward.

A lot of the stuff was actually junk. Old boxes and packing materials, foam and bubble wrap that Amanda lugged to the trash bin in the break room. She made judgment calls as best she could on the other stuff, what could go into storage in a patient room and what they needed to keep in the lab. She tried to pitch a box full of toys—souvenir bats, Styrofoam grenade launchers, etc. but Greg intercepted that and it stayed in the lab. Amanda did manage to preserve her own little work area by jamming it into a corner.

Greg interrupted her to tell her that he and Kenny had completed their equipment list and called it in. Greg wanted Amanda to change into something appropriate for the front desk and go up and staff it. He explained that, even though it was going on two in the morning, equipment would start drifting in, some of it scrounged up within the hospital and other stuff coming as high priority deliveries from elsewhere.

For the next few hours, carts full of equipment and supplies, pushed mostly by men, showed up at Glimmer's door. Some of the delivery people seemed confused about what was actually going on but others were totally business as usual. One young man was so delighted to find a new woman on his nightly rounds that she finally had to shoo him out.

Around four Greg came up from the lab and told her that there wouldn't be anything else coming. Amanda locked the door off the main hall and picked up the copies of the various receipts she had signed. The cart they'd used to transfer stuff between reception and the lab was about half full and she held the door into the ward so Greg could push it through.

About an hour later, one of the two men who had been shot in New York died. Greg and Kenny had the bed and equipment that had been Wickliffe's back in order and operational, and they put the man there.

They completed the initial surgery on the first corpse and had time to set up the other bed and equipment bay by the time the second man expired at 7:45 that morning.

CHAPTER
29

"I owe you both an explanation." Freddy Logan sat in his office in the Manhattan South Federal building. He wasn't sitting behind his desk. Instead he and Zeke and Jessica had pulled their chairs into an informal circle. The door to the office was closed.

"Zeke was with the coverage team on Andrianopoulos last night . . ."

Jessica interrupted, "I saw the overnight coverage report." She frowned. "Zeke wasn't on it."

Freddy nodded indulgently. "The report has been doctored. The whole episode is now classified."

Jessica's heavy black glasses had slipped down her nose and with her dark eyebrows raised above them she folded herself back into her chair.

"Leonard Andrianopoulos and Sam Arnold were shot on the street last night," Freddy said. "They were coming out of a restaurant and gunmen shot them down before the coverage team could react."

Freddy gave it a moment, ran a hand over his bright red hair before saying, "Zeke helped get Andrianopoulos and Arnold to the Manhattan Veterans Hospital. They're in a secure situation there, though neither of them is in stable condition."

Zeke wanted to hear the whole story, but he didn't think he would.

"There were four gunmen," Freddy said. "Two of them were dead at the scene and the other two are hospitalized in police custody. All four were connected to organized crime, and it looks like a simple hit. Somebody thought Andrianopoulos and Arnold were talking to the law and, of course, they were."

"Arnold wasn't." Jessica leaned forward.

"Not directly with our office but possibly with some other unit," replied Freddy. "We might hear about it." Then he said, "Our official position is that they are missing. The city police are calling the incident a shooting between gangs."

"How long are you going to hold them?" asked Zeke.

"We," said Freddy, "don't want the people behind the hit to know where Andrianopoulos and Arnold are or what condition they're in. We'll maintain they're missing for as long as it suits us."

"Can we do that?" asked Jessica.

Freddy raised his eyebrows. "Legally?"

Jessica shook her head. "I know we can't do it legally," she said. "Do we have hospital facilities where they can be cared for in secret? Do we have the clout with the city police and the press to keep it quiet? Do . . ."

"Yes," said Freddy. "We can manage it." He paused and then added, "It helps a lot that Zeke was on the scene. We were able to shut down information really quickly. It's a pretty small number of people who know what actually happened."

Jessica and Freddy both looked at Zeke and smiled. He nodded and looked back—an exchange of bows.

Zeke said, "Jessica and I were really counting on Andrianopoulos being brought into custody for extended questioning. How should we proceed without him?"

"I think," said Freddy, "that what we want to do is focus on Frank Russell. We have Osiris intelligence now that he met secretly with William Campbell before Campbell joined the administration. We also have, also from Osiris, the names of companies whose stock Frank traded illegally.

"I think we want to go back over everything we have on Frank and I think we want to search the restaurant."

Zeke and Jessica exchanged a glance. "Sounds good to me," said Jessica.

Zeke thought about Andy who also had an interest in Frank Russell.

CHAPTER
30

There were over a hundred wooden card tables in what looked like a onetime dance hall. The place was clean and utilitarian and almost all the tables were occupied by serious people playing duplicate bridge. They were in a separate world. Playing a game with an industrial process designed around it, an assembly line with rules and customs that each player had to know and obey.

Andy Crane sat across the table from his wife Elizabeth. The two of them had played bridge seriously early in their marriage but child rearing had sidelined them. Now that the children were older, Andy and Elizabeth had been thinking about playing again and Elizabeth had agreed to the evening although she knew that it was only a cover.

Judge Hardt, who had presided over Sarah Russell's trial and whose chambers Andy visited frequently, played regularly at this session with his wife. Andy wanted an off the record moment with the judge. He had, in fact, seen the judge earlier across the hall and had exchanged a look and a gesture to establish a meeting after the card playing was over.

As Andy got up to leave the table after the last hand of the session, the woman seated at his left tapped his arm and said, "Excuse me." She held the portable electronic scoring device that would enter the results of the hand into the club's computer.

Andy needed to press a key to indicate he agreed that the entered data was correct. After doing so, he said, "I'm sorry, we haven't played for several years. We're a little rusty."

The woman smiled and made a sort of sympathetic shrug but she didn't say "Welcome back".

Andy and Elizabeth went back around to the front of the club foyer where there were coat racks and a few chairs outside the club office. People were waiting there for the scores to be posted.

Judge Hardt and his wife were there too, standing alone. Elizabeth and Mrs. Hardt knew each other fairly well from various community and social activities. Mrs. Hardt gave Elizabeth a hug and said, "Joe and I were a little surprised to see you. Didn't you tell me you'd stopped playing when the children were born?"

"Yes," said Elizabeth. "We've been planning to start again, now that they're older. We'd forgotten how long and intense it is. We're both pretty wiped."

"I imagine," said Mrs. Hardt.

"How did you do?" asked the judge.

"Not very well, I'm afraid," said Andy.

There were quite a few people nearby. Small groups, some chatting, some not.

"Have you heard about Ear Mark Bridge?" the judge asked.

Neither Andy or Elizabeth had. Mrs. Hardt rolled her eyes.

"Well," said the judge, pleased. "It's just like regular bridge except," he paused, "the dealer picks up his cards and decides which suit, if any, he wants to be trump. Then he announces his decision and after that it's just playing bridge. Player to dealers left leads and player opposite dealer lays down his or her cards to make the dummy.

"Then dealer has at it. No limits on how many tricks can be taken and no performance requirements. Work it for everything you can get."

"How do you score?" asked Elizabeth.

"Dealer gets to count tricks taken."

"And Dummy?"

"Nothing," said the Judge. "It's not a team game." Then he brightened, "But it is an insider's game. You play four hands so everybody gets an ear mark."

The scores went up, and the crowd gravitated toward them.

Andy glanced around and decided that no one was eavesdropping. "I did want a word," he said.

"Should we drift off?" asked Mrs. Hardt, meaning her and Elizabeth.

The judge looked at Andy. Andy shook his head. "No, I don't think so."

He glanced around again, trying not to look furtive. "Do you remember that I mentioned Leonard Andrianopoulos the last time we met? He did a plea bargain on an uncharged crime."

"Vaguely," said the Judge.

"The feds made the deal, and they were going to take him into custody for interrogation but they put it off. They told us there was some administrative delay."

The judge nodded. Elizabeth and Mrs. Hardt were listening intently.

"Now he's gone missing," said Andy. "Just vanished. Nobody's got anything, not the city cops or the feds. Guy just vaporized."

Andy paused again, made sure no one was listening. "I know they were eager to get his testimony. It was stuff they really wanted and now it's just 'Gosh, guess he took off or something'. No big deal."

The judge thought a moment. "I know a guy. I'll send you his number."

CHAPTER 31

Leonard Andrianopoulos had suffered serious head wounds and Greg and Kenny had not been able to patch him back together enough to properly implant artificial cranial nerves into his brain. Post-animate-interrogation would be impossible in his case and they sent him back to the morgue. But the implants had worked nicely with the corpse of Sam Arnold and Sam turned out to be a gold mine of information.

Greg and Kenny were doing the interrogation and Amanda was working with the transcripts and voice files, putting the information together and organizing it as an Osiris document.

Arnold's testimony intrigued Amanda. His own activities were apparently limited to financial schemes, but he knew of a wide range of criminal activity. He talked about things like bank robberies and murders, and who controlled what area of the city's drug trade—and he gave names and dates.

Arnold did tend to run on, so testimony about one incident led to testimony about another. He also filled in the biographies of people he named. Who they worked with, who they hated, whose wife they were interested in. Sometimes it felt to Amanda like insider gossip. She struggled to pull it all together into some sort of logical document.

Greg came over with another stack of printouts and audio files. His last delivery was still in her in-box. "You going to be able to keep up?"

Amanda looked up, a little irritated. "What do you mean?"

Greg shook his head. "I just meant that it's really coming fast."

Amanda nodded. "Yes, and his testimony wanders all over. It's hard to get it straight."

"But it's not making you crazy?"

"Not yet anyway."

"Good." He turned and started back toward the corpse.

"Do we know yet who shot him?" asked Amanda.

Greg stopped and turned back to face her. "No. We haven't got to that yet. Every answer he gives leads to another question. We don't want to break up the pattern."

"Well," said Amanda, "I'll certainly be interested to hear how he got shot."

CHAPTER 32

Jerome Crosby was an employee of Morgan and McGown, the private investigation firm that Andy Crane did business with. Crosby came to Andy's office to report on the firm's investigation of Amanda Wilson's strange letter.

"There's a couple of odd things with your Ms. Wilson," said Crosby. "One is a company called Glimmer Development."

Andy had never heard of them.

"With the numbers off the check she sent you we were able to get access to her checking account," said Crosby. He was decidedly plump and seemed particularly comfortable with himself and the world. He had settled in a chair in front of Andy's desk.

"How did you do that?" asked Crane.

Crosby kept a straight face. "There's a vague but significant entry, several thousand dollars actually, under miscellaneous on your bill."

An intimation, Andy thought, that a bribe had been paid.

Crosby continued, "She's a government employee, she gets regular checks from the VA. She also gets regular checks from Glimmer Development."

Andy waited.

"Glimmer is a small medical research company," said Crosby after a moment. "They have a contract with the VA and they are located in the hospital at Goshen. From the regularity of the deposits, we're thinking that Amanda Wilson is providing them with some service. They're apparently quite generous."

"What do they research?"

"Something to do with artificial cranial nerves. Implantables." Crosby paused, shrugged his shoulders. "To tell you the truth, I really don't know what it's about. If you want, we could probably . . ."

"That's okay." Andy had his own in-office resources for researching corporate entities. "So, you think she's working with them?"

"Very probably," Crosby said. "She has an ongoing financial arrangement with the company and some sort of employment makes the most sense." He adjusted himself around in the chair, turning to face Crane a little more directly. "The other thing is that she's moved out of her apartment."

Andy straightened up a little, surprised, interested.

"Her rent and utilities are paid up," said Crosby. "Her mail is being forwarded. The apartment complex manager sees her come around once in a while with a young man to pick up stuff. He, the manager, thinks she's moved in with the young man—shacking up."

"Have you called either place? The hospital? Glimmer Development?"

"No," said Crosby. "You said be discreet. Phones can be tricky."

Andy nodded. He probably needed to talk to Amanda Wilson, and he had no idea of how to accomplish that discreetly.

CHAPTER 33

Reynolds, a forensic architect, led the way and Zeke and a computer technician followed him. They went back into the kitchen of Frank and Sarah Russell's restaurant and then off into the passages that ran to the store rooms and staff amenities. The corridors were narrow, the walls painted white, and the floors covered with green linoleum.

Freddy had spearheaded the plans for the federal search of Frank and Sarah Russell's restaurant. He had enlisted Reynolds and the computer technician from the office staff of experts. Those two had studied the building plans, acquired from the city, and decided where they wanted to start their part of the search. They seemed to know what they were doing, and Zeke had signed on to their little expedition.

The three of them stopped in front of a metal face plate built into a wall. The technician produced a screw driver and got started removing it.

"When they remodeled the private rooms," Reynolds said, "they rewired the one-twenty and added two-twenty. This cabinet is where they brought the new wiring for the three rooms together and routed it off toward the main system."

The face plate came off and exposed the electrical wiring in the cabinet. Reynolds spent a moment studying it and said, "These three cables are co-ax. They don't carry power, they carry things like video and audio."

"Could they be for big TVs in the private rooms?" asked Zeke.

"No," said Reynolds. "The circuitry for the televisions is in the ceiling. They're all controlled from a central location. The wiring drops down through the ceiling for the individual sets." He paused a moment and then added, "These cables are something else. They aren't on the wiring diagrams."

"I'm impressed," said Zeke. "Great find."

"Thanks." Reynolds nodded toward the technician. "He's got a wall scanner. We can follow the cables back into the private rooms. The scanner can see into the walls. We won't have to knock holes in them."

"We can if we have to," Zeke said.

The technician worked steadily along the walls. Zeke borrowed a step ladder from the kitchen staff and eventually they tracked the cable back into one of the private rooms. There, the scanner showed it going into an electrical junction box and several pairs of smaller wires coming out of the box. With the scanner they were able to track those and eventually they found the tiny cameras and microphones they'd been looking for.

"You'd never find them just searching the room," Zeke said.

"No," said the technician, "it's really good stuff. And it's all hard-wired so it's low power consumption. It wouldn't show up much, if at all, on a bug sweep."

The three stood in silence a moment, impressed with what they'd accomplished. Zeke said, "Let's go back to the cabinet and trace the cables to the other end."

Reynolds lead the way back. The three coax cables that came into the cabinet separately from the three private rooms were fastened together with tie wraps and routed out in a bundle. The bundle was easy to track, and using the wall scanner they worked their way to a closet with a false back. Behind the false back the cables emerged from the wall and were plugged into a small computer server which had a rack for removable hard drive cartridges. There were six cartridges in the rack.

"It looks like these cartridges are it," said the technician. "There's no connection going out to the wide world."

"So somebody comes in and swaps out the drives," said Reynolds.

"Yes," said the technician. "They've got two drives for each room. When one gets full the computer should switch to the second. Somebody swaps a new one in for the full one."

"Like collecting eggs in a hen house," said Zeke. He was thinking about where the collected drives ended up. "How many people are involved, do you think?"

Reynolds looked at the technician. The technician looked up at the ceiling, considering. "I think two or three, just to have somebody available if the system needed attention. And they'd have to be trained to some extent or another. Whoever set it up really had to know what they were doing."

Zeke thought that was probably correct. "Any idea about the capacity on these disks?"

The technician took a moment before he said, "This is good equipment. It would depend on the quality of recording they want. I'd say at least a couple of thousand hours each."

"Those rooms probably don't average five hours of use a day," said Reynolds.

"This stuff most likely went in when they did the remodel of the private rooms—four years ago I think? Even so we're not talking about a box car full of hard drives."

Zeke knew what the others did not. He knew that Frank Russell had secretly sold a piece of the restaurant to some shady people in order to finance the remodel of the private rooms.

CHAPTER 34

"I'm a little surprised you wanted to meet here," said Andy.

His guest was a man named Mallory, a city police lieutenant. He was a thin man, not very tall. They were sitting at a small table in Andy's office.

"It's a big anonymous city," Mallory said. "I'm not important enough to rate a tail."

He'd said as much on the phone. He'd called to introduce himself as a friend of Judge Hardt's—said the Judge had asked him to call Andy.

Mallory had offered to come to the office and when Andy said that he himself had a tail Mallory had asked the circumstances and then the name of the agency Andy employed. None of that deterred him, and now here he was, sipping coffee the admin had provided.

"Judge Hardt says you're interested in what happened to Leonard Andrianopoulos," he said.

Andy explained that he represented Andrianopoulos in a criminal case.

Mallory looked him over carefully. "The judge trusts you—and I trust the judge. This is serious business."

"I can imagine," said Andy.

Mallory smiled. "I'm not sure you can. Leonard Andrianopoulos got shot coming out of a restaurant. People he'd done illegal things with thought he might be going to talk. A guy named Sam Arnold was with him and Andrianopoulos's former friends shot him too, for good measure I suppose."

Mallory gave Andy a moment to think about that before he continued. "This little shooting went wrong because neither the shooters nor their employers knew that there was a substantial team of federal agents watching over Leonard Andrianopoulos."

It had occurred to Andy that feds were possibly watching his client. Freddy Logan kept putting off the date for Andrianopoulos to come in and surrender. Freddy said there were internal issues in the prosecutor's office, but if they were trolling Andrianopoulos around . . .

"There was a well-equipped surveillance van," said Mallory, "a chase car, and four or five more people on the ground.

"When the first city squad arrived they found two of the shooters dead and two others seriously wounded. Andrianopoulos and Sam Arnold were also badly wounded. The Federales had the scene in hand. Word came down to the squads that it was a no news site."

"Were you there?"

"No," said Mallory, "but I did the report . . . well, I prepared the report for burial."

"Any idea why they wanted to cover it up?"

Mallory spent a moment getting his thoughts together. "I think it's possible they wanted to keep the condition of the victims secret."

Andy raised his eyebrows.

"They took the victims to the Veteran's Hospital," Mallory said. "The shooters all went off to the local city hospital in an ambulance but the Feds wouldn't let them take Andrianopoulos and Arnold. They held them until an ambulance from the Veteran's hospital arrived."

"So they take them to the Veteran's Hospital because it's a federal facility and they have better control there," said Andy. "Easier to keep the condition of the two men secret. Easier to protect them?"

"Could be that," said Mallory.

Veteran's Hospital tugged at Andy's memory and he remembered Amanda Wilson up in Goshen.

Mallory didn't seem to have anything to add. Finally, Andy asked, "Any way you think I can get more information?"

Mallory shrugged. "Talk to the feds."

"I don't think that will work."

"The two shooters who survived are talking as fast as they can, trying to save their lives. But the city cops have them sewn up tight."

Andy frowned.

Then Mallory said, "You might try the guy in charge of the ambulances that came from the city hospital. He was apparently pretty upset about the way the Federals were doing things."

"You think he'll talk to me?"

"He might. I'll get you his name and contact information."

CHAPTER 35

Amanda tried to interrogate Sarah Russell about Sam Arnold but she didn't have much luck. Greg came over to help. Sam had become their star attraction, and they wanted to get Sarah's assessment of him—a sanity check.

Amanda gave the corpse a shock in the way Kenny had shown her and asked again about Sam Arnold. Finally, Sarah answered.

Sam Arnold is a wannabe. He hangs around our bar and buys drinks for anybody he thinks might be a gangster. He's a good listener, and he laughs at everybody's jokes. Frank says he's a white-collar criminal with blue-collar aspirations. He wishes he was tough enough to be a thug.

The voice trailed off and Amanda applied another shock. When Sarah didn't respond, Greg nudged Amanda aside and applied a stronger jolt. Sarah Russell cried out and Amanda winced, but the voice resumed.

Arnold knows devious people in the financial sector and he helps make contacts. He thinks he's a kind of insider at the restaurant because he and I have done some business.

When the voice stopped, Greg got ready to apply another shock.

"Wait," said Amanda. "Let her rest a minute."

"I'm a doctor," said Greg. "This is what I do. Don't tell me how to do it."

"Oh, a doctor. That makes it okay. Step aside for Mr. Doctor."

He paused and stared at her a moment. "You don't have any trouble with the title of 'Mrs. Doctor'."

Taken aback she stared at him. "What does that mean?"

"Well," he paused. "You aren't a nurse but you look like one . . . and you act like some."

She stared at him again, this time holding his gaze. "So I'm out to marry a doctor?"

He smiled contemptuously, turned on his heel and walked away.

With her face set in a scowl she turned back to Sarah Russell. She twisted the shock knob sharply . . . too sharply . . . too hard. Sarah screamed and Amanda shrank back, appalled at what she'd done.

Sarah started to speak.

Martha and I were supposed to call Mom's boyfriend Joe. I knew he was a congressman but I couldn't mention that and I specifically couldn't tell Martha.

Joe paid for a nice apartment and the rest of a nice life style. We even had a nanny. Mom was stunned at her good fortune and convinced that we were moving up the class ladder. She got something of a handle on her substance abuse level and she took the nanny's word as law. Nanny picked out our clothes, corrected our manners, and filled us with tales of how 'nice people' did things.

Joe was, of course, married and actually lived in another, even better, part of town but that didn't bother Mom. I think that summer was the only time I ever saw her actually happy.

And then Sarah's voice trailed off. Amanda realized that Greg and Kenny were standing by her.

"Where the hell did that come from?" asked Greg.

Amanda sheepishly admitted what she'd done with the high-power shock.

Greg's mouth opened and he started to speak but did not. Instead he paused, then finally said, "The memory could be linked to the pain."

"But it doesn't seem a painful memory," said Amanda.

Kenny rubbed his chin. "It could be a kind of consciousness. Like she's telling us something she wants us to know."

Greg straightened up and raised an eyebrow. "Consciousness from where? The new cell growth?"

"But I thought that was autonomous," said Amanda. "Like when the government collapses but the grocery stores are still open and the garbage is still getting collected."

"Well," said Kenny. "That's kind of what happened when the Roman Empire collapsed. Eventually new governments did develop."

CHAPTER 36

"This is such a shift in content," said Freddy Logan. He set a new packet of Osiris material on the edge of Zeke's desk and then rolled one of the guest chairs in Zeke and Jessica's small office to the corner by the white board. "We're not sure how we should handle it." He nodded toward the Osiris material with emphasis.

Zeke wondered who the mysterious "we" were, but he knew better than to ask.

"The other material was usually centered around a particular group of people and some particular activity," Freddy said. "But this stuff . . . this stuff is all over the place. Some of it is about things that happened thirty years ago. There are bank robberies and murders—Ponzi schemes."

He took a moment, letting Jessica and Zeke catch up before he continued. "There is more data here than the three of us can handle so we're going to spin off another unit."

"Where?" asked Jessica.

Freddy smiled, "Right now that's on a need to know basis, Jessica, and . . ."

"We don't need to know," said Jessica.

"No." Freddy smiled again, gently shaking his head.

"So we're fired," she said.

Zeke knew precisely who those "we" were.

Freddy leaned back in the chair and spread his arms. "No, no, no." He looked at Zeke. "We're just going to spin off another investigative unit."

He stopped there, giving the others a chance to speak. When nothing came he said, "We've got a good start on the link between Secretary Campbell and the Stophonix market manipulation and we will continue to pursue that. And this stuff you've turned up at the restaurant with Frank's equipment! That's amazing and who knows where it will lead."

Zeke did want to discuss the material from the Russells' restaurant. "That's not going to be easy. We have thousands of hours of video from Frank's equipment to analyze. We don't know who most of the people are and conversations are jumbled together. We don't even have an efficient set-up for pulling the data off the hard disks."

"And we think there must be a big cache of disks somewhere," said Jessica. "We think they were recording for several years."

"Well," said Freddy, "we're in luck there. We're getting a nice budget boost so we can afford some really good resources to help with organizing and analyzing the material."

Zeke found that reassuring and Jessica brightened a bit. Freddy seemed to sense it. "We're growing," he said, wrapping up, "and you two are certainly going to grow with us."

He waited a moment and then got up from his chair. "So, go over this and let me know what you think." He stepped to the doorway and paused. "Give some thought to what sort of resources you want for working with the drives from Frank's equipment."

When he was gone, Jessica said, with her big black glasses centered on Zeke, "Lucky for you."

He looked up. "What's lucky for me?"

"That we weren't fired. If we had been it would have been your fault."

"What?"

Jessica explained. "Well . . . all of those doubts you had. All of your pious little observations on ethics."

"You don't get fired for expressing your honest concerns," he said.

She laughed. "When you get back to your home planet, you're probably going to want to write a report."

Zeke let that go. He did have a serious issue he wanted to discuss. "I think this business of Frank's equipment . . ."

Jessica quietly shrieked. "If I hear one more reference to Frank's equipment."

He gave her a questioning look.

"Frank's equipment . . ." She looked at him with arched eyebrows and exasperation.

He thought a moment. Then he said, "You mean like how something can have two different meanings—one regular and one about," he shrugged, "sex?"

"Double entendre?" she said.

"Maybe you just have . . ."

"I do not," she said.

"Okay," he said. "Frank's *surveillance*," he searched for words. He settled on, "The surveillance installation in the Russells' restaurant."

She smiled. "Thank you."

"Well," Zeke said. "I don't think that the surveillance installation belongs to Frank. He's a smart guy, but he doesn't have the resources. That setup requires professional level technicians and they have to be well-paid enough that you can trust them with a clandestine operation. I think it's much more likely an operation of George Thornton's."

"George Thornton the mob guy?" asked Jessica.

"The mob guy according to the Osiris Source," said Zeke. "If that installation was operated by George Thornton and friends we aren't likely to find the stash of disks."

Jessica nodded tentatively in agreement.

They settled into reading the new Osiris material and found it, in fact, quite different in scope and content. They had been reading for about an hour when Jessica looked up. "I've seen Sam Arnold mentioned a few times in this stuff. We never saw him mentioned, before did we?"

"Maybe once or twice," said Zeke. "But nothing substantial about him in Osiris until I dropped him all shot up at the VA hospital in Manhattan."

"They even have Sarah Russell's opinion of him in here," added Jessica.

Zeke hadn't read that yet. Jessica found the page for him. He read it and shook his head. "Do you have any idea what's going on?"

"Nope," she said.

They usually took a coffee break in the late afternoon. About three Jessica stretched and got up. Zeke closed his computer files and slid back his chair.

"It does make you wonder though, doesn't it," she said. "This double entendre stuff."

"What does it make you wonder?" asked Zeke.

"Makes you wonder what they were talking about when they invented language," said Jessica.

CHAPTER
37

"See that kid in the powder blue shirt? The one with the pencil thin mustache and the blue lensed glasses."

"I do," said Andy Crane. They were in the offices of Morgan and McGown, the agency that Crane employed to do his investigative work. Morgan and McGown had called and said they had things to report—could Mr. Crane come by.

Mr. Crane did come by and sat in a video presentation room viewing pictures on a huge television screen.

"We voted him most likely to be the picture taking, drug dealing snake in our little garden," said Natalie Wang, the presenter for Morgan and McGown.

Surprised, Andy asked, "You think it's a student?" Then, "You think it's a drug dealer?"

"Yes and yes," said Ms. Wang. "Makes sense, doesn't it? Your local representative of organized crime. Small time perhaps, small potatoes, but..."

Andy shifted in his seat, intrigued. "And that's the guy?"

"Oh no," said Natalie. "That's just a teenager a bit taken with himself... if you can imagine such a thing!" She said this tongue in cheek, literally. It was an interesting effect.

Ms. Wang's associate, Jerome Crosby, the operative who had

earlier brought Andy the Morgan and McGown report on Amanda Wilson, seemed comfortable in the role of associate. He alternated between pleasantly polite and deeply concerned as the moment required it.

Crosby controlled the video presentation, and he brought up another picture. This time a taller boy, lanky. He wore wire-framed gold glasses and had an oddly endearing smile. He stood on the steps at one of the entrances to the school Andy's children attended. "This is our guy," said Crosby

"This kid?"

"Yes."

Andy had a hard time visualizing this kid taking the casual pictures of his children that had so terrified him.

"We think the school probably looks on a small time drug dealer as a necessary evil," said Natalie Wang. "We think this one is more evil than they bargained for."

She showed a video of the kid pretending to talk on his phone but actually taking pictures of other students. "He's probably documenting his customer base."

"He also has a weakness for pretty girls. We expect he's hoping for a wardrobe malfunction," Crosby said with a hint of a leer.

Andy, thinking of Olivia, was not remotely amused.

"We're a little divided on what to do about him," said Natalie. "At first we thought let him ride and keep an eye on him. But as we watch him, we think he's too dangerous to let run around."

"You think?" said Andy with an edge of irritation in his voice. It occurred to him that they were interested in the young man as a sort of case study—watching him evolve from an iffy kid into a junior gangster.

Natalie apparently caught his tone and adjusted her own. "Yes," she said promptly. "The photos he took of your children were clearly used for criminal purposes. Who knows where else his work is showing up."

"And his drug inventory is picking up too," said Crosby. "We're pretty sure he's got prescription opiate pain killers now and plain old heroin when you can no longer afford those."

"So . . ." asked Andy.

"So, we're going to have a discreet word with the local police," said Crosby. "They can bust him for distribution without any indication of our being involved."

"And his picture taking?"

"We think bringing in the photos might link his arrest to you," said Crosby.

Andy mulled it over, not quite content.

"Selling heroin to school children is still pretty serious business," Natalie said. "He'll be in plenty of trouble."

Andy nodded, conceding the point.

"We'd like to maintain surveillance," said Crosby. "We want to see if our kid gets replaced."

Andy agreed with that. Then he asked, "Is there anything else we should be doing?"

Crosby and Ms. Wang exchanged a long look. Natalie Wang said, "No. We think, in fact, that the situation is better than we had feared." She brought the picture of the kid standing on the school steps back up. "This young person is disturbing and disgusting. But he is not a professional criminal. He was included in this to scare you, nothing more. And now we're going to get him out of the picture."

Morgan and McGown were expensive and Andy used them a lot. More than ever now he hoped they were worth the money.

CHAPTER
38

"*I always get less spades than you guys,*" said Martha. She smacked her freshly dealt cards down on the table. "It's not fair."

We were playing three handed spades at a patio table by the pool. It was early afternoon and Mom hadn't called—not the night before and not that morning.

"Do you remember the rule for that?" asked Nanny.

Mom not coming home for the night wasn't unusual. But, at least since the congressman had come into our lives, she'd been better about calling and letting us know when she planned to be home.

"The rule for not getting enough spades?" asked Martha skeptically.

That struck me, too, and I turned my attention back to the table.

"No," said Nanny quite seriously, "for using less and fewer."

I stifled a laugh and Martha looked away so Nanny couldn't see her roll her eyes.

"Fewer people, less gin," said Nanny and then laughed herself. "Or less gin, fewer people. It works either way."

Martha picked up her cards. "Okay," she said, "I always get fewer spades than you guys." Then she added, "It's still not fair."

"Amusing?"

The voice startled Amanda, and she stopped laughing. She turned away from the corpse of Sarah Russell and found Greg standing behind her. She started to explain but caught herself and stopped.

She and Greg hadn't exchanged a kind word since the "Mrs. Doctor" incident. When that had happened her first instinct was anger at Greg for accusing her of being a social climber or a gold digger. Then she began to wonder if he thought that she was only interested in him because he was a doctor. When she had tried to broach the subject it had settled back into a childish standoff—who'll blink first.

"Have you got a minute?" He motioned toward the other side of the room where he and Kenny were interrogating Sam Arnold. "We're going to ask about the night they were shot."

She hesitated, unsure what he meant.

"I know you have concerns about how Arnold and Andrianopoulos died," he said. "I want you to hear."

Amanda nodded and turned off the interrogation equipment she had been using. Then she went over to Arnold's bed. Kenny asked the questions and Arnold talked about finishing up dinner with Andrianopoulos. He described the two of them leaving the restaurant, the polite bunching up around the door, then out into the night. When a man nearby in the dark made a sudden move, Arnold instinctively stepped back. He saw several flashes of light and fire. He heard shots as he fell to the sidewalk.

And they got no more than that. Arnold had no idea who the shooters were or even that he and Andrianopoulos had been the targets. Kenny asked the questions two or three different ways but didn't get any more information.

Amanda started to inch away. She didn't think further interrogation would get them better answers. But Greg caught her eye and signaled softly with his hand for her to stay put. She knew what he was doing. He wanted to let Kenny have all the time he wanted to try to get an answer.

She was glad Greg had done that, though it did no good. Kenny got no more answers and when he gave up and started shutting down the interrogation station he said, "We don't know who shot them. It could have been the government."

"Yes," Greg conceded.

Kenny finished shutting down and then went off, back to his room or maybe the cafeteria. Greg looked at Amanda and shrugged. She thought he had done the right thing, and he was being the adult in the room but she was still a little too angry to speak a kind first word and let him win their standoff. She nodded politely and went back to Sarah Russell, powered up the equipment there, and restarted the interrogation session.

Nanny made us a late lunch, but I wasn't hungry. Normally she would have badgered me into eating something but that day she didn't.

Martha had finally begun to worry, too, though she was worried that something had happened to Mom, that she was somewhere hurt and couldn't call.

That worried me, too, but I was more worried that the bad old days were back.

Martha always claimed she remembered a lot about those times but she didn't. She had been too young and most of the time she hadn't understood what was going on.

I knew the only thing Martha really remembered was being scared and having to keep quiet. And that did happen. There were times when Mom disappeared for days and left Martha and me alone in some old, creaky apartment. Sometimes with no food and sometimes with food but we were too scared to eat.

I remembered laying awake at night listening to the neighbors fighting. Shouting and cursing and sometimes shots. I also remembered the men Mom brought home and the screaming matches and the times Mom went to the hospital because a screaming match degenerated into a domestic disturbance.

"You girls don't need to worry so much," said Nanny. "There are a lot of perfectly good reasons why your mother hasn't called."

But I could feel the bad old days coming back. There was a knot in my stomach and my face tingled. My hands trembled, and I clinched them into fists to control them.

The corpse of Sarah Russell moved. Sarah's fingers curled in ever so slightly as if trying to grip.

"Please help me," came out of the speakers. The voice was different. There was real fear in it. "Please help me."

Amanda administered a shock. Sarah moaned but then the moan faded to sobbing. "Can't you help me? Please . . . can't you help me?"

CHAPTER 39

"You know what you need to do first?"

It was Reynolds, the forensic architect, and Zeke Keele was pretty sure Reynolds was going to tell him what he should do first.

"You should measure it," said Reynolds. "Take the house plan and go out there, or send somebody out there, and measure it. If there really is a secret room, the numbers won't total up right."

"We're pretty sure there's a secret room," said Zeke. He had the Osiris source.

He and Jessica got a warrant, put the Russells' beach house under guard and set out to do the measuring themselves.

The road in the neighborhood of the Russells' house was a narrow blacktop. It ran along a steep earthen bank of five feet that separated the town from the beach. Most of the houses on the beach side of the road had open wooden stairways out back that lead down to the ocean. In contrast, the Russell house was marked by a mail box on a post and a driveway that dropped off sharply and twisted its way toward the beach.

Zeke and Jessica drove down to the house and parked the car. When they got out of the air conditioning they were met by a warm salt breeze and the low rumble of waves breaking onto the sand. The house, with dark gray shingles and crisp white trim, was built on a low rise in the beach. It was one story with several long screened porches.

"Feels like a thousand miles from the city," said Jessica.

Zeke agreed.

The guard let them in and they walked around the house and compared the floor plans with the actual building. They decided to start measuring in the kitchen. It was at the northwest corner of the house and it looked like it would be one of the trickiest. Zeke took off his suit coat and loosened his tie.

When they'd been at it for an hour Zeke said, "This feels a little domestic."

"Pardon me?" said Jessica. She had taken off her own jacket and parked her high heels. She worked barefoot on the polished wooden floors.

It reminded Zeke of when he'd been married. "It's like we're measuring for curtains—planning to paint."

"Well," she took a long look around the room, "if you owned *this* place that might be an actual possibility."

He smiled at her, confused.

She smiled back and shrugged.

When they finished the measuring they did the arithmetic and found about fourteen feet missing on the north/south axis and around twelve on the east/west.

They walked around the house with the floor plan and were able to get a pretty good idea of where the secret room was, but they didn't try to get into it. Instead they came back the next day with the forensic architect, Reynolds, and the electronics technician who had been with them at the restaurant.

The two experts quickly focused on a bit of blank wall on an interior hallway. They found and tripped a latching mechanism and opened the Russells' secret room. Zeke and Jessica followed Reynolds and the electrical technician in. The room was, like the rest of the house, a 1920s period piece. There were comfortable chairs, a table, and a discreet wet bar.

Jessica looked it over and confided to Zeke that she was a little disappointed. "I expected more of a 'secret room'."

He laughed. "Use your imagination. Powerful, sophisticated people in hidden discussions—maturing their felonious little plan."

She looked vaguely perplexed and nodded.

Reynolds and the technician found microphones and two cameras in the walls. "This stuff is adequate, but it's not nearly as sophisticated as what we found at the restaurant," Reynolds said.

The electrics technician agreed. "You can get this kind of stuff at a big box store."

"It's clunky, but it'd do the job," said Reynolds. "They didn't have to worry about hostile, probing eyes in here."

They followed the wires through the wall with the scanner. It led them pretty quickly to the floor.

Zeke and Jessica moved about together, keeping out of the way.

"They're looking for a priest hole," said Jessica.

"A what?"

"A priest hole," she said. "When Elizabeth was suppressing Catholicism in England, a lot of Catholics would have a secret place where they could hide a priest if they had to."

"I thought the Tudors suppressed Protestants," said Zeke.

"That was the previous queen."

Zeke brightened. "Mary Queen of Scots?" he ventured.

"No, Mary Tudor," she said. "Bloody Mary." She shook her head slowly and looked at him as if he were an utter moron.

Reynolds and the technician were having a serious discussion over a patch of floor. Zeke edged over to them. "What'd you find?"

"A space," said Reynolds. "The covering is heavy and we can see a lot of metal under the floor. We think the mechanism to open it is probably radio controlled."

"So you need like a remote," Zeke said.

"That," said Reynolds with a nod, "or drill into it and pop it open."

Zeke and Jessica exchanged a look.

"Pop it open," Jessica said.

"I don't like to do it that way," said Reynolds.

"Why not?" asked Zeke.

"Paperwork mostly. Usually the department has to pay for repairs. There should be a manual override somewhere."

"And it's not elegant," said the technician, smiling. "That's what he really doesn't like."

"I think Jessica's right," said Zeke. "We need to pop it."

The technician went back outside to their van for some heavier tools. Reynolds started in again with the scanner on the floor. When the technician got back, they began drilling holes and then enlarging them with a thin-bladed power saw.

They worked on it for twenty minutes. Then the technician said, "Here's the radio receiver. I think we just have to short out this switch." There was a loud "snap" and the smell of electrical smoke. The technician looked up with a sheepish grin. They heard a motor whir. The rectangle of false floor dropped down and slid left out of the way revealing a small metal staircase.

Reynolds took a flashlight and went down the stairs. The technician followed with a flashlight of his own and a tool box. They found switches and turned on lights. Jessica went down tentatively with Zeke behind her.

The "priest hole" was six-by-six and had a low ceiling. The walls and floor were bare concrete. Against one wall there was a long table supporting a computer and four heavy plastic stand-alone cabinets.

The computer was configured as a server. Reynolds and the technician agreed that it was totally adequate for recording and controlling the microphones and cameras they had found in the secret room above.

"I don't see any keys for these cabinets," said Jessica.

The technician produced a drill from his tool box and inquired with a shrug. Jessica looked at Zeke.

"Let's get them open," he said.

The first cabinet had shelves stacked with tape cartridges. There were a couple of different types of cartridges and each one was individually labeled with a date range.

"I suppose they changed cartridge type whenever they upgraded the server," said Zeke.

Jessica studied the labels on a handful of cartridges. "There are notes on some of these."

"Probably an index somewhere," said Zeke. "On the computer . . . maybe a little black book."

"It's a gold mine," said Jessica.

"Will this be admissible in court?" Reynolds stood behind them, looking over their shoulders.

"That'll be tricky," said Zeke.

"But it's great intelligence," said Jessica. "Lots easier to figure out what's going on if you know where the bodies are buried."

The second cabinet had more cartridges of various sorts, all stacked neatly and labeled. The third cabinet was half full of disk cartridges like the ones they'd found at the Russells' restaurant.

"Oh my," said Reynolds.

"Didn't we think the disks at the restaurant were going to Frank's silent partners?" asked Jessica

"Frank was probably making copies for . . ." said Reynolds.

"His personal use," said Zeke.

"Yes," said Reynolds, "easy enough."

"I think we need to get Frank into custody," said Zeke.

Jessica laughed. "Protective custody."

CHAPTER
40

Andy Crane had exchanged selfies with Mark Butler.

Butler was an ambulance crew chief. He had been on the scene the night Leonard Andrianopoulos got shot.

And the selfie trick worked. When Andy came into the South Street Saloon he saw Butler sitting alone at the bar with a tall beer in front of him. It was mid-afternoon, and the bar was nearly empty. Andy took the next stool and ordered a beer.

"Andy Crane?" asked Butler.

"Yes," said Andy. His own beer came, and he paid for it.

Butler nodded and the two of them took their drinks and went to a booth along the wall.

The bar was small and dark but it was clean and the price of the beer suggested it was discreetly upscale and probably did a lot of business nights and weekends.

"A friend of mine asked me to get in touch with you," said Butler when they were seated.

Andy sat for a moment and then realized that Butler wanted him to supply the friend's name. "I met with Lt. Mallory," he said.

"How do you know Mallory?"

"A mutual friend." Andy did not think it prudent to mention Judge Hardt.

Butler seemed to relax. "Mallory said you're a lawyer, and you were representing one of the men who was shot."

"Yes," said Andy. "I was representing Leonard Andrianopoulos."

"Okay," said Butler. "How'd those two do? Did they make it?"

"I don't know." Andy took a moment to organize his thoughts. "The federal prosecutors claim they have no idea where Andrianopoulos is or what happened to him."

"And you don't want to call them liars."

"Not unless I have to and not unless I can prove it."

Butler took a drink of beer. "I know there were two men shot in an ambush. I don't know their names or even what the fight was over. I got the three wounded shooters loaded up but there was a federal guy in a suit and he wouldn't let me take the two victims. I talked to the NYPD guy in charge of the scene and he said his orders were coming from way up the chain of command and he was to let the federal people make all the calls."

Andy thought there might be more. He bought another round. "This is a nice place," he said.

"It is," said Butler. "It gets a little busy on weekends."

The beer came, and they drank in silence a moment. Butler said, "The law is that the first priority is the health of the injured persons. Those two guys were bleeding in the street. I had EMTs in a well-equipped ambulance and mine was the nearest hospital. He should have let me take them."

Andy knew that Butler, and/or the hospital he worked for, had a financial interest in collecting patients, but it didn't seem to Andy that that was what Butler had been thinking about.

"I know they have priorities too," said Butler, "and I know there are more important things in the world than some low-life bleeding to death. But . . ."

Andy nodded—in agreement that Butler was stating the intent of the law correctly and that he himself understood how it felt when the world reminded you of your own powerlessness.

Butler continued, "Lt. Mallory said that you and some other friends of his think something big is going on but you're running out of leads."

Andy said, "Yes."

Butler took out his smart phone, pushed some virtual buttons and slid it across the table.

There was a little triangle pointing to the right. "What's this?" asked Andy.

"Dash cam video," said Butler, looking a little smug.

The video showed a street scene. It was night and there were police cars, uniformed officers and others in plain clothes. Andy could see Butler having an apparently serious discussion with a man in a dark suit. That man was Andy's friend Zeke Keele.

CHAPTER 41

Greg and Kenny had been interrogating Sam Arnold in alternate shifts and Amanda's in-box had been perpetually in overflow. The only questioning she had done of Mrs. Russell was to cross check or flesh out areas in Sam Arnold's testimony.

And then they found an infection in one of Arnold's still unhealed gunshot wounds. They couldn't stop it and reluctantly they had pulled the plug and sent the corpse off to the morgue. Kenny had left town to see his brother and sister—there were some issue with his mother's estate. Gregg took the opportunity to try and catch up on maintainance and documentation. Amanda was finishing up her transcripts. With a little time on her hands she planned to interrogate Sarah Russell about the day at the pool, the day Sarah's mother hadn't called.

She was powering up the equipment when she saw Greg coming across the room.

"Could we talk a little?" he asked.

"Okay," she said. She suspected why he might finally be swallowing a little pride and venturing into making up. With Kenny off with his family Greg and Amanda were alone in the Glimmer ward. Amanda herself was not opposed to at least a possible truce.

"I don't know what you're so mad about." Greg seemed genuinely perplexed.

"You really don't know?" asked Amanda.

"Mrs. Doctor . . ." he ventured.

Amanda frowned. She'd had to acknowledge to herself that she had actually thought about being 'Mrs. Doctor.' Well, not exactly 'Mrs. Doctor'. More about being 'Mrs. President and CEO of Glimmer Development.' She believed the company would make a lot of money and could bring a lovely home in an elegant suburb, social status and children in private schools. But she didn't let Greg off the hook just yet.

He continued. "I just said that because I was mad. I didn't mean it."

"Lots of people believe you say what you really think when you're mad."

"No," he said, "when you're mad you say what you think will hurt the most." He paused a moment. Then he asked, "So what are you so mad about?"

"Well," she said, standing up straight. "Let's see." She locked her eyes on his. "You're manipulative." They maintained eye contact. "You treat me like I'm stupid. You ask my opinion and then disregard it if you don't agree."

When he didn't respond she went on. "You play little games, like this week of not speaking that we just went through." She smiled prettily. "Enough?"

He shrugged slightly, inviting her to continue. She did.

"I'm not always sure that you are telling me everything you know from the government contacts."

He nodded and took a moment before saying, "I don't tell you everything word for word and I don't always give you all the details. But I tell you and Kenny everything important. I'm not keeping anything from you."

For the most part she believed him. It was Kenny's theory that Greg hid things from them.

"What about the other stuff?" she asked.

He tilted his head, inquiringly.

"You think I'm stupid. You're manipulative." She rattled off his sins. "You never really take me seriously."

Greg thought again before he answered. "I'm sorry. I don't think you're stupid and I don't mean to be manipulative." He sat down on the edge of Sarah Russell's bed.

"My parents were old fashioned, really old fashioned. My father was a physician—no one at our house ever said doctor—and my mother was a homemaker. My father couldn't iron a shirt and I never saw him so much as make coffee.

"I didn't have sisters, but I had two brothers. Mom was sort of shut out. She cooked and cleaned and had her friends. She was always loving and supportive, and we certainly loved her, but she just wasn't interested in the same things we were. She had her world, and we had ours."

Amanda understood that.

"I'm better than I used to be," Greg said. "I didn't think of girls as really thinking . . ."

Amanda dropped her jaw in exaggerated shock.

"I mean not thinking like I do."

Deeper and deeper, she thought.

"Anyway," he said, "I'm sorry. I regret that I wasn't more aware of or interested in what they were thinking or feeling." He got to his feet. "I'm particularly sorry that I've been that way with you sometimes. I know better now."

And so they made up.

Later she returned to Sarah Russell and started an interrogation session. Amanda brought it back around to the afternoon by the pool and she asked when Sarah's mother had finally come home. Sarah said her mother had not come home or called. That evening Nanny had received a couple of phone calls. The next morning she packed Sarah and Martha up as cheerfully as she could and took them to their grandmother's. Sarah never saw or heard from her mother again. Nobody called the cops and Sarah was sure she saw Nanny pass a bundle of cash to Grandmother.

And then Sarah's voice shifted. It was clear and sharp and Amanda could hear the fear in it. "Please help me," she said. "Can't you help me?"

The voice startled Amanda. She went to get Greg. When she got back with him Sarah was quiet.

"You said her mother hadn't come home," said Greg.

"Yesterday's news," said Amanda. "Her mother never came home. The nanny took the girls back to their grandmother the next day."

"When did they see their mother again?" he asked.

"Never."

Greg's eyebrows went up. "Never?"

Amanda nodded.

"Did they call the police?"

"No," she said. "They never reported her as missing."

"And the rich boyfriend was a congressman?"

"Yes, that's what Sarah said."

Greg moved around to the microphone. "Do you mind if I ask her some questions?"

"No," said Amanda.

Greg started questioning Sarah Russell. He got back to the incident and began probing for details—the location of the nice apartment, the date her mother went missing, the congressman's real name, where did Grandmother live?

Amanda stood at the bedside, following the interrogation. She was surprised to notice that Sarah Russell's right arm had grown so much that the restraint was cutting off circulation. There was a strap around the cushioned restraint that held it fast. A clip on the strap controlled the tension and Amanda reached down and loosened the clip to adjust the strap. The corpse jerked powerfully and its right arm came out of the restraint. Amanda shrieked and stepped back, her eyes wide.

The free arm swung violently, going for the restraint on the other wrist. Amanda fell backwards onto the empty bed behind her.

The corpse's free right hand undid the restraint on the left wrist and the legs began kicking furiously. The left hand came free and the dead woman sat up.

Amanda rolled across the center bed and off the other side. Greg came running around the foot of the bed and put his arms around her.

One of the legs ripped out of its restraint and swung wildly, splattering blood from the flesh scraped raw by the restraint. The arms tried to get at the restraint on the other ankle but the free leg thrashed about so violently that the hands couldn't do it.

Greg and Amanda huddled together behind the center bed. Reluctantly she looked up at the scene. Blood flew from the flailing limbs in great arcs and the corpse screamed.

"The hands are working together," Greg said, "but the legs aren't cooperating. The face looks like it's on it's own too." There was fear in his voice but not panic.

Using both her arms, the dead woman pulled the IV pole next to the bed and hoisted herself up with it. The legs cooperated finally, and the corpse stood up in the bed. It continued to bleed profusely. The TPN port had ripped out as had the connections to the heart-lung machine. Wires ripped from the various monitoring devices hung loosely from the crouched, quivering corpse.

The physical development was wildly disproportionate. The arms and legs were muscled like a weight lifter's but the torso remained the slim, elegant body of Sarah Russell.

And then Amanda noticed the face, drifting above the body, stuck onto the grotesque creature like something in modern art.

Amanda started when she saw that Sarah Russell's eyes were open and her face was animate. Amanda had often observed the face, contemplated it, seeking to know more about Sarah. It was a lovely face, but it had never flinched, never lost its repose of sleep or death. Now the face was alive with movement. Her mouth shaped words and her eyes were open and bright. Even in this terrible circumstance Amanda could see the charm and magic of Sarah Russell. And though Amanda could not make out the words Sarah was trying to say, she could see clearly that the blind eyes were pleading.

Amanda turned to Greg. "What can we do?"

Greg shook his head. "There's nothing we can do. Even if we could get her under control we probably can't stop the bleeding. We could never get the life support hooked back up in time to save her."

And he was right. Within minutes the dead woman's movements

quieted down. Then her legs gave way and, like a toddler, she plopped back down on her bottom.

She leaned back and, with her head on the pillow, she closed her eyes and whatever spark there was went out.

CHAPTER 42

"I understand that, Dr. Conklin. But we have to be able to prove it."

Kenny was a little frustrated. He had spent a lot of time on the foundation's secure web site establishing who he was and what he wanted to do. He had traveled to New York to meet over dinner with foundation representatives Josh and Marissa. And now they wanted proof. "Pictures?" he asked. "Video?"

"Of the talking corpses?" asked Marissa with a hint of disgust in her voice.

Josh laughed awkwardly. "We're used to dealing with document dumps."

When Kenny had sought out a way to blow the whistle on the government's secret use of Glimmer technology he had searched the dark internet for an organization to work with. His choice of the foundation that Josh and Marissa were attached to had been based largely on intuition. He had not checked for "type of stuff leaked".

But given that, he knew he had to get a hold of himself and calm down. It was not the time to get snippy.

"A demo, even if we could pull one off, wouldn't do it," said Josh. "It'd be too easy to fake, nobody would believe it."

Kenny agreed. Then he remembered the hand-off package. "Actually, we do have some documentation," he said. "The plan was that at some point we would hand off the operation to government people. So we have this collection of documents, kind of like a technical manual. It's not that well organized, but all the information for taking care of the corpses and running the interrogations is in there."

Josh's face lit up with curiosity but only for an instant. "Do you think it's enough? Do you think the government people will be able to pick it up just from the hand off documentation?"

"They could but it wouldn't be easy," said Kenny. "We planned on staying on for a transition period."

Josh and Marissa exchanged a look. Marissa asked, "How do you get the artificial nerves? You don't have a factory do you?"

"We send the specifications to a sub-contractor," said Kenny. "They actually manufacture the nerves."

"And the specifications are in the hand-off package?" asked Josh.

"Of course," said Kenny.

Josh thought a moment. He glanced again at Marissa. "That could do it," he said. "The experts could look at it and verify that the technology would work."

That made sense to Kenny, too. And it wouldn't be hard to get. He'd just go back to the ward, wait for an opportunity to grab the hand-off documentation and walk out with it. He relaxed a bit and looked around the restaurant.

"We should probably go back to the apartment," Josh said.

"Yes," said Marissa.

Kenny didn't understand that. "Why? I'll just go back up to Goshen and, when I get a chance, I'll grab the stuff and come back down with it. It's all on a thumb drive."

"Well," said Josh, stretching the word out. "We need to firm up plans and we can't really discuss details here. Plus, we should probably call the foundation."

Kenny shrugged. "Okay."

"Might want to pick up Rachelle too," said Marissa.

Josh nodded and smiled. "Yes," he said slowly. "Paperwork. There is some, and she's good at it."

"What paperwork?" asked Kenny.

"This is serious business, Dr. Conklin," Josh said. "You're going to be famous . . . infamous. You're going to have to leave the country for a while at least. The government may try to put you in prison."

Kenny knew that was true, and he resolved again to calm down and keep his head in the game.

Marissa reached forward and squeezed his forearm.

They left the restaurant and got Josh and Marissa's car from the valet. It was a small, expensive, dark blue two-door. Kenny squirmed into the tiny back seat and twisted around so he could fasten the seat belt.

They picked up Rachelle at her apartment and with what amounted to a shove from Marissa they got her into the back seat and into Kenny's lap. Fortunately she was small and managed to get herself turned around and buckled in. By scrunching to his right Kenny was able to wedge his left shoulder back between them and against the seat.

Rachelle sighed. Then she took Kenny's left wrist, lifted his left arm up over her head and draped it down around herself. "It's a 'French' car," she said as she snuggled against him.

"A 'French' car," echoed Kenny.

"Yes," said Josh from the front seat. He gave the make and model.

As they drove north into Manhattan, with the lights of the city flowing past and Rachelle comfortably tucked in next to him, Kenny decided he quite liked "French" cars.

"HAVE YOU GOT AN UP-TO-DATE PASSPORT?" asked Rachelle. She was working with Kenny on the odds and ends, cleaning up the details.

"I do," he said, a little confused. "But I thought you would be experts at that sort of stuff."

They had been at Josh and Marissa's apartment for about an hour and Kenny realized he had probably been drugged. He was awfully calm and content and the world had a nice glow. He decided it was probably for the best. It would take a little time for him to adjust to the fast lane life of international freedom and openness-crusader-slash-whistleblower.

"We are experts at a lot of things, but it's one less thing to take care of," Rachelle said. "What about the others, Dr. Ellerby and Ms. Wilson?"

"He does, I know. I'm not sure about her."

Rachelle thought a moment. "Amelia sounds really nice . . ."

"Amanda," said Kenny.

"Yes, Amanda," said Rachelle. "She does sound nice, but she's not really critical to the operation, is she?"

Kenny shook his head. "If she doesn't come, Greg won't come."

"Oh," said Rachelle. "So they're like a couple?"

"Yes."

"So we'll need a contingency." She was sitting cross legged on the floor and she made another note in her small leathery looking notebook.

Marissa had gone off in a taxi to get a rental car, the little French car wouldn't do for this job, and Josh was somewhere in the apartment trying to make fake magnetic identity cards modeled on Kenny's Goshen hospital ID.

Kenny's plan to just go back to the hospital, wait for a chance to grab the hand-off package and bring it back to Josh and Marissa had not survived review. The project would be too big to depend on haphazard timing. There would need to be resources on hand ready to pick up and run with the material and Kenny would need to be installed in a safe environment. In addition, Kenny wanted to talk to Greg and Amanda and bring them with him. If they were opposed to what he was doing, and he couldn't swear they wouldn't be, they could detain him or have him arrested. So the plan had changed. Marissa, Josh, Rachelle, and Kenny were going up together in the rental car, use the fake pass cards to get into Glimmer, get the stuff and put the proposition to Greg and Amanda. If those two declined or resisted they would tie them up. When Kenny and his new partners were safely on the way, someone would call the hospital and tell them to go let Greg and Amanda out of whatever restraints they were in.

"We've got a problem," said Josh. He was coming back from the kitchen with Kenny's ID card held in his right hand. "This card is pretty well done. I don't think I can duplicate it myself. They're doing something odd with the background colors and the magnetic encoding is different than what I've seen before."

Rachelle moved from the floor to a chair. "Can you work around it?"

"I'm going to take it to the Finnigans. They're really good with this sort of stuff."

"Finnigans?" asked Rachelle.

"Remember the little electronics shop? The brothers lived in the back?"

She shook her head.

"We had a party there. They had a whole bunch of virtual reality stuff to play with."

"Oh, yeah," said Rachelle. "I remember. The VR party. Those guys were brothers?"

"Yes, they say they need to work with the card. There are several encryption schemes and the Finnigans think they can figure out which one to use by looking at this one."

"How long will it take them?" asked Rachelle.

"Couple of days. Could be longer."

It seemed to Kenny that the Finnigan brothers should be able to do a rush job for international freedom and openness-crusaders-slash-whistleblowers.

"So we're going to be on hold for a while," said Rachelle.

"Yes," said Josh.

Kenny had another thought. "What about the car? How long will Marissa reserve it for?"

"I think two weeks," said Josh.

"If you bring the car back early or late, aren't the fees pretty high?" said Kenny.

Josh looked perplexed.

"Kenny," Rachelle said with a warm, indulgent smile. "We're not taking the car back."

CHAPTER 43

"And you got this about a month ago?" asked Zeke Keele.

Andy Crane nodded. He had given Zeke the note he'd received from Amanda Wilson. The note that had come to his house disguised as a birthday card for his daughter Olivia. Zeke and Andy were in a booth at Third and Long, getting started on a pitcher of India Pale Ale.

Zeke, still looking at the letter, said, "So this is where you got the information about the Russells' deal on custody of the children."

"Yes."

"And you think it was accurate information?"

"Frank Russell thought it was accurate."

A faint smile crossed Zeke's face. "Why didn't you show this to me before?"

Andy took his time. "I didn't know about your interest in Veteran's Hospitals then," he said. "I hadn't seen the video of you with Leonard Andrianopoulos and Sam Arnold when they were lying shot in the street."

Zeke paused, looked around the bar, topped off his glass. When he spoke he made no acknowledgment of what Andy had said. Instead he asked about the letter. "What do you know about Amanda Wilson?"

"She is a federal employee at the VA hospital in Goshen," said

Andy, ready to get down to business. "But she's apparently assigned to support Glimmer Development, a contract organization located in the hospital. My investigator thinks Wilson has moved into the Glimmer ward at the hospital and that she has a separate financial arrangement with the company."

Andy continued, "Glimmer is small. Their only facility is at Goshen. They are doing research into artificial cranial nerves. They get a lot of federal money through somewhat vague channels."

"And you got information from Amanda Wilson that you would think only Sarah and Frank Russell knew," said Zeke.

"Yes. And we're both pretty sure that Sarah Russell is dead."

"So we should maybe drive up to Goshen and talk to Amanda Wilson."

Andy had a slightly better idea. "I'm pretty sure Judge Hardt will give us a search warrant . . . in case Ms. Wilson is reluctant."

That was an escalation that Zeke had not considered. It took him a moment, but in the end he said, "Okay."

CHAPTER 44

It was late evening and Amanda and Greg were working in the lab. They had the doors propped open to get some circulation, and they heard somebody in the hall.

"Must be Kenny," said Greg.

Amanda nodded. Kenny had been off visiting his family and was due back.

A man and a woman waving pistols and wearing masks burst into the room. "Hands up," the man shouted. "Hands up now."

The pistols had long extensions on their barrels and they struck Amanda as the rolls in comedy skits out of which unwound a little flag that said "bang." She was, in fact, thoroughly confounded. She knew there was some talk of security issues but she never really believed . . .

And then Kenny came through the door. He had a sort of silly grin on his flushed face. A second masked woman came behind him.

Kenny raised his hands and motioned for everyone to calm down. "This isn't what you think."

"Damn, Kenny," said Amanda, "they've got guns."

"Guns with silencers," said Greg.

Kenny frowned. "It's complicated." He raised his hands in front of him and blurted out, "We're going to leak the project."

Amanda and Greg exchanged a look of disbelief.

The masked man said, "We want to have Dr. Conklin in a safe place when this information is published. He wanted to offer you the chance to join him . . . us."

Amanda was scared and she felt betrayed, but mostly she was angry at Kenny.

"So is your mother really dead?" she asked.

Kenny's jaw dropped a little, and he stared at Amanda. He seemed hurt. "Yes," he said finally.

"You're high," said Greg.

Kenny shrugged. "I probably couldn't have handled all of this otherwise."

"What'd you take?" asked Greg.

"I don't know."

Greg gave him an inquiring look.

"I just realized I was high, and I figured it was for the best."

"So your new friends here just slipped you a little something uninvited," said Greg.

"You shut up," said the man with the gun.

"Your new pal's going to shoot me Kenny," said Greg. "You'll need a safe place for sure then."

"Cut the crap," said the masked man.

Greg smiled at him with a smile Amanda had never seen before.

"Hey," said Kenny. "Everybody calm down." He straightened up suddenly. "Where's Sarah Russell?"

"She died," said Amanda.

"What?" Kenny was stunned.

Amanda looked at Greg. "It's complicated," he said. "She got out of the restraints and stood up."

"All the life support was pulled loose," said Amanda.

"How can that be? They've never done anything really but regurgitate memory."

"This was different," said Amanda.

"No idea what's going on?"

"No," said Greg. "We'll get an autopsy report."

Kenny nodded. "Probably want them to have a neurosurgeon take a look."

"Absolutely."

Kenny turned to the masked man. "Josh, I think I'm going to stay here."

"What?"

"I'm going to stay here. This is pretty interesting."

"No," said the gunman, whose name was apparently Josh. "You can't change plans now."

Kenny shrugged. "With the documentation you can go ahead and leak it."

"No."

"Our plan is screwed anyway," Kenny said. "Pictures of Sarah Russell would have proven that the government is executing people and then sending them here. Without pictures of her . . ."

"If you don't come I'm going to shoot your friends," said Josh.

Kenny looked at him in disbelief.

"I don't think he plans to leak the story, Kenny," said Greg.

"Shut up," said Josh.

Greg didn't. "With you and the hand-off documentation he can set up a lab of his own. Maybe sell the technology to some 'interested party'. Worth a lot more than a couple days' headline in some big shot newspaper."

Josh raised his gun and pulled the trigger twice. Greg staggered and fell down.

Josh took a step forward and raised the pistol again.

Amanda knew he was going to kill Greg. With tears streaming down her face she flew against Josh, throwing her fists against anything she could hit.

He held her off, his hands up in mock defense and mock terror. Then she landed a lucky right that hit him just below the check bone, glanced and broke his nose. He staggered back, startled. There was a souvenir bat on the table. She snatched it up and swung it hard into the side of his head. He slumped back. She stepped forward and hit him again.

There was another *phhtt,* and a bullet slammed hard into the wall behind her.

CHAPTER
45

The division's garage was on Foley Square. Zeke Keele checked out a car a little after 9:00 a.m. He picked up Andy Crane and the two drove north along the Hudson to Washington Heights. There they crossed the bridge and headed north-northwest toward Goshen.

CHAPTER 46

"If he dies he won't be the only one," said the tall woman with the gun. She stood just behind Kenny and she said it softly, almost under her breath.

Kenny knew her name was Marissa, and he knew the other one, the smaller woman wearing a mask and holding a metal basin for Josh to throw up in, was Rachelle. But he didn't mention either name aloud.

In truth, Josh had nothing much left to throw up but his stomach still retched up a little liquid and he moaned in agony. He had been unconscious much of the night but he was in and out of it now. He needed to be moved to a head trauma unit and Kenny said it again.

"No," said Marissa. "You fix him"

Josh roused and repeated the "No." Then he said, "We're walking out of here."

In the next bed over from Josh, Greg squirmed with pain. Kenny had gotten the bullets out of him and sewed him up but they didn't have much in the way of pain killers on the ward. Greg was restrained so he couldn't hurt himself thrashing around, and that would have to do. Beyond him Amanda sat tied to a straight back wooden chair. She was gagged and Kenny had watched her through the night. Occasionally she nodded off but mostly she was awake with her eyes wide in some varying degree of fear.

"What about them?" asked Kenny.

"We'll leave them like they are," said Marissa, "and call the hospital when we're clear."

"He's not stable enough to leave alone," said Kenny, indicating Greg.

"Well, you're going to have to get him stable enough."

Rachelle sat the metal basin down with authority and moved to the foot of Josh's bed. She pulled off her ski mask and dropped it on the table. She had a small, precise face with a wide mouth. She looked awfully young. "I'm leaving."

"I'll shoot you dead," said Marissa.

"You can't spare the bullets," said Rachelle.

"Want to bet your life on that?"

"Let her go," said Josh. His voice was weak, and he strained to make himself heard. "She didn't know what she was getting into."

"No," said Marissa. "We need her."

"Let her go," repeated Josh.

The two women stared at each other a moment.

Kenny said, "There's a bus stop just outside of the main door where we came in. Turn right and you'll see the shelter."

Rachelle quickly fussed her hair into remarkably good shape and kissed Kenny on the mouth. "You are a dear man," she said solemnly. Then she opened one of the double doors, stepped through and slammed it shut.

CHAPTER 47

Andy and Zeke discussed the situation as they drove. Andy told Zeke all he knew and Zeke had told Andy all he thought he should tell him. They had traveled in silence through the bright fall foliage in the Schunemunk Mountains and into the valley of a small stream east of Chester. Traffic was spaced out nicely and moving at a stately pace.

There was something tangential that Andy wanted to know and he decided the time might be right. "What's it like to work for Freddy?"

Zeke didn't answer right away. Finally he said, with a faint smile, "Just like working for anybody else. Nothing special about Freddy."

Andy sighed. "Aw, Zeke, we've sort of crossed the Rubicon here. Besides, I'm not a gossip."

Zeke thought about it a moment and then relented. "Do you remember when they first started rolling out traffic cameras in force?"

Andy nodded.

"We were at some office thing, a dinner," Zeke said. "Some of us were talking about it before the speakers started. We were pretty impressed with the number of tickets they were writing and the way they were dropping speeds and incidents in the stretches of highway they were targeting."

Andy remembered, but he also remembered the accompanying civil liberties debate.

Zeke continued. "Freddy thought the people in charge had made a mistake. They got a burst of good publicity and they did prove they could significantly improve driver behavior when the cameras were in place.

"But Freddy argued that they should have kept quiet about the cameras. He believes generally that most problems are caused by small numbers of people who consistently and willfully misbehave. The cameras were secret eyes, and they were all connected to computers. If the police had used them to spot the really bad drivers they would have had a target list. Drivers that they could give 'extra' attention. Had they done that they could have made a significant improvement in the character of the motoring public before the cameras went into general use."

Andy looked around. They were crossing a small river. From the bridge he could see the highway ahead winding gracefully up into the colorful hills. He didn't know what to say.

CHAPTER
48

"Have you got a wheelchair?"

Startled, Kenny took a moment. Josh's clarity of mind had been all over the map since Amanda hit him. Now he spoke clearly and purposefully. Kenny said, "There's a supply closet up by the nurse's station. There's one in there."

Josh nodded slightly.

The lighting in the lab was dim, and the air was sticky. Josh lay in the center bed. Marissa stood to his right—a damp cloth for his forehead in one hand, a cocked pistol in the other.

Greg moaned, semiconscious in the bed behind her.

"Go with Kenny and get the wheelchair," Josh said.

Marissa's face brightened a little, and she nodded.

Josh asked, "You've got the thumb drive safe?"

Marissa nodded again and patted a small, buttoned pocket over her left breast. The thumb drive held the documentation set for Glimmer's Post Animate Interrogation technology.

"Good." He gave her a thumbs up.

Kenny did not repeat his physician warning—that Josh, because of his head injuries, should not be moved. Josh and Marissa were reckless but Kenny knew they weren't stupid. They were gambling that they could move Josh more or less safely and escape jail and possible death for a life of wealth and underground fame.

And, chillingly, Kenny could see no advantage for them in leaving witnesses.

In that vein, and equally disturbing, Marissa was no longer making eye contact with Kenny, and she neither looked at or referred by name to either Greg or Amanda.

Sweat soaked Amanda's clothes and dripped off her forehead and into her wide frightened eyes. She had tried working her wrists loose and failed. She could rock the chair she was tied to a bit but that would lead to her tipping over and being even more vulnerable.

During the night Kenny had pleaded with Marissa and finally got Amanda a bathroom break. Marissa had tied Kenny up and then taken Amanda at gunpoint down the hall to the restroom. When they came back there were cuts on Amanda's face. They were small, and they didn't appear to be very deep but they were fresh.

"When you're back," said Josh, "we'll call a rental place and get a van."

Marissa nodded and motioned with her gun for Kenny to get moving. He finished adjusting Josh's position and set the wireless remote back down on the bedside tray.

The supply closet was at the other end of the hall, up near the locked door that led to reception. Marissa walked a little behind Kenny. "You have no idea what this stuff is worth, do you?" she said. "With this, there are no secrets anymore."

Kenny actually did know that. There were no secrets as long as you were willing to track down and murder whoever you thought might know them.

The door to the supply closet was not locked, and the wheelchair was stacked against the back wall. Kenny got it unfolded and back out into the hall.

Marissa continued talking erratically but her eyes never left Kenny for more than an instant and the pistol muzzle followed him relentlessly.

When they got back into the lab, Josh used Marissa's phone and called and arranged to rent a wheelchair-accessible van. "Forty-five minutes," he said when he had finished the call. "They're going to call when they get close."

"So . . ." She tilted her head and smiled.

"So when they call we'll get me into the chair. When we're safely away we'll call the hospital and tell them to go untie Kenny and his friends."

"We will," said Marissa solemnly.

CHAPTER 49

There were acres of parking lots surrounding the Veteran's Hospital at Goshen. The hospital towered over them like a small mountain.

Zeke Keele and Andy Crane were behind one of the small circulator buses that roamed the campus road network, moving passengers between their cars and the main building. Zeke and Andy eventually found a visitor parking zone and got a slot reasonably close to the main doors. The circulator buses stopped on the right side of the entrance and the city buses stopped on the left. The doors to the building were set behind a row of imposing columns.

Zeke and Andy checked in at the front desk and a guard led them back to the security center to present their warrant. There they waited ten minutes before a young woman took them to the office of the head of security. Inside that office they found Freddy chatting with a large man in a khaki uniform.

Freddy looked up. "You didn't really think you could get a warrant at Second Manhattan without me knowing about it did you?"

Neither Zeke nor Andy expressed surprise.

Freddy continued, "And you brought our old friend Andy Crane." He extended his hand.

Andy took the proffered hand. Old acquaintances was a better characterization of the relationship between Freddy and him. They had faced each other several times in federal court and had avoided any personal animosity.

"We've had your search warrant sealed," Freddy said. "As officers of the court you are bound to silence on this. Are you both okay with that?"

Andy knew when he agreed to come along on the execution of the search warrant that he was essentially embedding himself with the feds. He nodded his assent to Freddy's question as did Zeke.

Freddy nodded in response and turned to the man in uniform who he introduced as Calvin Sims. "Cal is head of security here and Glimmer Development's guardian angel."

As they shook hands, Sims said to Zeke, "Freddy says you're coming on board."

"Apparently," replied Zeke.

Freddy had them sit down. Calvin Sims went to get some coffee.

"Do you know who William Chu is?" asked Freddy, looking at Zeke.

"The name's familiar but . . ."

"He's deputy chief of the criminal division in St. Louis now. Two years ago he was working with a whistle blower program. He stumbled onto a little medical device company, Glimmer Development, they were working on a very interesting technology.

"Bill and I had worked together before and we had a shared frustration with getting at white collar crime and corruption. He called me and a couple of other like-minded individuals. We made a deal with Glimmer and set them up here as a skunk works operation."

Sims came back with coffee and some cups.

"Up until now," continued Freddy, "we've had a skeleton crew working on the project. The two doctors who developed the technology and a federal employee here in the hospital who's moonlighting for them."

And that's my Amanda Wilson, thought Andy. He sipped his coffee and tried not to betray his excitement.

"It's been a remarkably effective operation." Freddy spoke with near reverence. He paused briefly, took a breath and then continued. "But now we're going to present it to the agencies, get it on the black budgets. We'll need government staff and . . ."

"What does the technology do?" asked Andy.

Freddy turned, apparently surprised at being interrupted. He smiled. "They can interrogate dead people. They wire stuff into the corpse's head and access the brain like a data base."

"They can do what?" asked Andy, his voice filled with incredulity.

FREDDY FINALLY STOPPED TALKING and the four men started off through the halls of the hospital. Cal Simms, the head of security, in his khaki uniform and Freddy, with his bright red hair, drew a certain amount of discreet attention. When they entered the Glimmer receptionist's office the young woman on duty was surprised. Cal showed her the search warrant and pointed at the door to the interior. The receptionist shrugged her shoulders and Cal stepped forward and entered a universal code.

Beyond the heavy door they found a long hall leading back into the gloom of the ward. Sims sniffed the air and stopped. "You smell gunpowder?"

The other three men sniffed dutifully. "I think so," said Zeke.

"I think so, too," said the head of security. He drew a pistol. Freddy and Zeke produced black automatics from their shoulder holsters.

Sims shouted. "Anybody in here? We're security. We have a warrant." He paused briefly and then repeated the message. There was only silence in response. "Zeke," Sims said, "you stay in the hall. Freddy and I will check out the rooms."

Andy was relieved to be left out of the strategic planning. He didn't have a gun, and he wasn't comfortable with them. He stayed behind Sims and looked for light switches. He flipped on each one he found in the hall and in the rooms that Freddy and Zeke had cleared.

Slowly the team worked their way to the double doors at the end of the corridor. Cal cracked one open. There were lights on in the room beyond.

"Anyone in there?" shouted Sims. "We're security. We have a warrant."

A man moaned. Then a woman shouted.

Sims flung open the door and he and Freddy burst into the lab. Zeke and Andy followed quickly.

Andy got through in time to see a tall woman with a long barreled pistol drawing a bead on another woman bound in a chair. The chair rocked side to side—teetering.

Freddy, Zeke, and Cal all raised their guns but the tall woman was a heartbeat ahead of them. She had her shot lined up but as she fired the chair toppled over and the three pistols of the government men exploded in near unison. They echoed in the small room like cannons. The woman who had fired pitched sideways and small, bloody chunks of her flesh tore away.

No one spoke or moved. The smell of gun powder hovered over the sick room stench of the lab. Sounds were vague and far away. Freddy threw up.

Andy crossed the room to the woman in the chair. The bullet had missed her as she fell. He got her upright and undid her gag. "I'm Amanda Wilson," she stammered. "I'm a federal employee."

"I thought so," he said. "I'm Andy Crane."

The woman looked up and her mouth dropped open with relief. Her eyes were wide and dry with fear and exhaustion but she ventured a tight-lipped smile.

"These patients need more help than I can give them," said a short man with a bushy dark beard and long dark hair. He stood between two of the beds with his hands up. Zeke stood there too—gun still drawn.

Cal Sims got out his phone.

Freddy wiped his mouth with a shaky hand. "Are we going to be able to keep this secure?"

"Absolutely," said Sims. "I've got good people."

Andy turned back to Amanda. "What happened here?"

She spoke with difficulty. "The man with his hands up is Kenny

Conklin, Dr. Conklin," she said. "Dr. Greg Ellerby is in the bed on the right. Kenny came here with the man in the wheelchair and a couple of women. Kenny thought they were going to gather facts and publish them—blow the whistle."

She took a moment, rubbing her wrists where the restraints had been. "But they just wanted to steal the technology. Greg figured it out and started to fight and that man shot him."

"The man in the wheelchair?" asked Zeke.

"Yes."

"What happened to him?"

She stared straight into Andy's eyes and said. "I hit him . . . with a bat." She didn't look sorry.

He helped her to her feet, and they went to the bed where Greg Ellerby lay. "How is he?" she asked.

"I think he'll be okay," said Kenny, who was still standing between the beds with his hands up, "but he needs pain killers and rest." He turned to the man in the wheelchair. "But this guy . . . Josh . . . he has a really serious head injury. He needs an emergency room for starters."

Several security people and a couple of EMTs with a gurney came into the lab. The latter loaded up the dead woman. That made Andy remember. "Didn't you say there were a couple of women?"

Amanda nodded.

Zeke perked up. "Another woman? Where is she?"

Two doctors and a nurse came in. At Kenny's direction they went to work on Josh and Greg.

"She left," said Amanda.

Freddy joined the group.

"Where did she go?" Zeke asked. "What was her name?"

Amanda shrugged. "Kenny," she said with a slightly raised voice. "Do you know the name of the other woman? The one that left."

Kenny looked up and glanced around the room. "No."

"Do you know where she went?" asked Zeke.

Kenny glanced around again before he spoke. "No."

Amanda shrugged again. "I think she may have taken a bus."

"A bus?" asked Freddy.

"A city bus. She left not too long before you got here."

"What did she look like?" asked Zeke.

"She was pretty," said Amanda. "Had short black hair. Seemed awfully young." Amanda stroked Greg Ellerby's forehead.

Freddy moved back toward the center of the room and Zeke and Andy moved with him.

"I guess this will blow the lid off," said Zeke.

Freddy raised his eyebrows. "This?"

Zeke nodded. "If the guy in the wheelchair . . ."

"Josh," said Andy.

"If he lives," said Zeke. "And then the woman who left . . ."

Freddy shook his head. "Those aren't the biggest problems. We're going to present all this stuff to select congressional committees to get funding."

"But those are secret proceedings," said Zeke.

"In theory they are—but there will be leaks and rumors. Same with Josh and the missing woman—rumors."

"Well?" asked Zeke.

"Well," said Freddy, "we'll start our own rumors."

Zeke raised his eyebrows and frowned.

"How long you been hearing about black helicopters?" asked Freddy.

CHAPTER 50

"He glitters a bit," said Jessica. She meant the man from Washington who stood next to Freddy Logan on the low step up stage. "It's a nice touch."

The man from Washington was Freddy's boss. The two of them were addressing the new MAAT team in a small auditorium on the third floor of the Manhattan South Federal Courthouse.

There were about a dozen people scattered in the front three or four rows of the small auditorium. Zeke and Jessica sat alone in the last of the occupied rows off to the right. Their invitation to the meeting had been unexpected and had arrived at the last minute.

The other seats in the auditorium were occupied by members of the new MAAT team. Jake and Jessica's interaction with the group had been limited. They'd met a few of the members but others were just faces glimpsed in the halls.

The MAAT team was picking up the investigative portion of the expanded and reorganized Osiris project. Another group of government personnel was taking over the Glimmer post-animate interrogation operation at Goshen and a secret congressional oversight committee was being organized to monitor Osiris end-to-end and approve its black box funding.

Zeke and Jessica had been spun off into their own group. They were getting all the audio and video from the Russells' restaurant and beach house and the resources to exploit them.

"I want to acknowledge Zeke Keele and Jessica Miller," said Freddy. "They played a big part in getting us to where we are today with this effort. They're getting a group of their own. Zeke will head it up and Jessica will be his deputy. They have a pile of solid gold intelligence to work through." He motioned for Zeke and Jessica to stand. "They'll be making headlines."

They stood up together and exchanged a slightly sheepish look.

Freddy turned to the man from Washington and Zeke and Jessica sat back down.

"Now that you're going to be so important," Jessica said after the awkward moment had passed, "maybe we should glitter you up a little."

The man from Washington wore a dark gray suit. Gold rimmed glasses, a gold lapel pin, and gold cuff links produced most of the glitter. He did not, as was generally expected on these sorts of occasions, launch into an elaborate and official blessing of Freddy and the new group—breaking a symbolic bottle of champagne against a symbolic prow.

Instead, in a tone just short of 'reading the riot act', he talked about the other new group. The new internal working group that would put ethical guidelines in place and have the authority to ensure that they were adhered too. He shot an occasional glance at Freddy.

Freddy, seemingly unaware of the personal attention, looked as grim as the boss and regularly nodded enthusiastic agreement.

Jessica nudged Zeke and asked in a whisper, "Isn't your friend Andy Crane in that working group?"

"He is," said Zeke.

"But isn't Crane sort of a crusader bunny?"

Zeke took a moment before he spoke. "He is a little. But he's pro-equal justice. He's not pro-crook."

That seemed to satisfy her. She gave Zeke a long look and asked, "Would you wear cuff links?"

CHAPTER 51

It rained at Sarah Russell's funeral. It was cold and overcast and the leaves were starting to fall in numbers.

Andy Crane walked along with the crowd of mourners moving along the cemetery's narrow lanes, going from the graveside back to their cars.

Martha Simonson was there with her husband and the oldest of their two daughters. They were on the other side of the lane, just ahead of Andy. The little girl was five or six and she walked along quietly with her parents—very serious in a dark blue frock coat.

"Mr. Crane."

It was a woman's voice. Andy turned. It took him an instant to realize that the three people behind him were Amanda Wilson and the two doctors from Glimmer Development. He was a little startled by how nicely Amanda had cleaned up since the horrible day on the ward at Goshen. The doctors looked much better too, although Greg Ellerby had an arm in a sling.

They stepped down a gravel path to get out of the foot traffic. Their four umbrellas made a canopy over their little group.

"Wasn't that Sarah's sister, Martha, just ahead of us?" asked Amanda.

"Yes," said Andy. "Her and her husband and the oldest of their little girls."

"It's amazing how much she looks like Sarah."

"It is," said Andy.

"I'm so glad we could come," said Amanda.

"Yes," said Greg, and Kenny nodded. "We really feel like we got to know her."

"We did get to know her," said Amanda.

They stood quietly for a moment. Then Greg asked, "How did you get the body released?"

"When Frank Russell was arrested," explained Andy, "he agreed to give custody of the Russell twins to Sarah's sister Martha."

"Like he promised," said Amanda.

"Yes," said Andy. "So Freddy Logan's office worked out a compassionate release to simplify the custody change. Releasing the body made Sarah officially dead so Frank alone could sign over custody."

The wind picked up and the little group shifted a bit to minimize the chill. Andy thought about moving on but he sensed that the others wanted to talk some more.

"Did they ever find out anything about the foundation?" asked Kenny.

Andy wasn't sure what he meant.

"The foundation that Josh and Marissa worked with," he said. "We're a little worried that we might be on a list of theirs."

Andy thought about what he could or should say, applying Freddy Logan's "need to know" policy. He made a judgment call, expanding 'need to know to do your job' to include 'need to know to keep your sanity.' "There was no foundation," he said. "It was just Josh and Marissa and a website." Josh was still hospitalized, but he had been interviewed and Andy had seen a partial summary of what he'd said.

"What about the others?" asked Kenny. "The woman who left, the guys who made the magnetic IDs?"

"Apparently they were independent operators," Andy said. "It seems to be a sort of entrepreneurial type environment."

"Well, that's good to know," said Greg. "I mean, we've got good security, really good security now, but still . . ."

"Oh," said Andy. "You must have started training the transition team?"

"Yes," said Greg. "There are only three so far but they are extremely good. The facility is going to stay at Goshen but we've been moved to a bigger ward."

"And we don't have to live there," said Amanda. "And we're working normal hours."

"Well, more normal," said Greg.

"How long do you think the transition will take?" asked Andy.

"A month," said Greg.

"Could be two," said Kenny. "Then we're going to go somewhere and get started in the implantable nerve business. Start doing something for living people."

"Putting all those crooks away was doing something for living people," said Greg.

"Any idea where you're going?" asked Andy.

Greg shrugged. "One day it's Atlanta, next day it's Minnesota. We have no idea."

Andy got ready to wish them luck and move on, but Amanda asked, "Have they done anything about Sarah's mother disappearing?"

"Yes," said Andy. "They've had a couple of long interviews with Martha and I think they're getting ready to turn it over to FBI cold case."

"What did Martha think?"

"She's torn," Andy said. "She's touched that their mother may not have deserted them, but if she didn't desert them then she's probably dead."

"She didn't desert them," said Amanda. "At least Sarah didn't think so and she was there."

The grim conviction in Amanda's voice made Andy think about how much she and the two young doctors had seen. "You three have been through some really traumatic stuff." He didn't mention specifically Kenny's bringing in Josh and company and very nearly getting them all killed. "It's good to see you coping and moving on."

Amanda smiled and hit Kenny in the shoulder with a punch that was not altogether collegial. "We're getting there," she said.

ABOUT THE AUTHOR

Dan earned a living by doing minor league journalism, technical writing and finally computer programming.

But he had been called Dan after a character in a science fiction novel by his very young parents and that bit of predestination stuck.

At seven he decided to be an artist and settled on painting. Two or three weeks into that he realized he didn't draw very well and he switched to literature.

In middle school he encountered his first serious library and discovered H. G. Wells.

A few years later a pair of chortling school pals found a copy of the novel *Skin and Bones* on the shelves of a local thrift store and stuck it in his locker - a comment on his physique.

Dan read the Thorne Smith novel and had the second of his science fiction heroes.

An interesting and challenging pair to emulate, H. G. Wells and Thorne Smith. *War of the Worlds* meets *Topper*.

And then in high school Dan's still young parents were having drinks with friends before going out to dinner. He was in the kitchen, mulling over a typewriter. A woman in her middle thirties, looking for the bathroom, stumbled across him and asked what he was doing. He explained.

"I started out to be a writer," she said. After a pause she added, "Never quit."

The regret and poignancy in her voice was such that he never did.

ACKNOWLEDGEMENTS

Anna Lawrence for providing a sounding board and occasional sanity checks.

Her husband, David Lawrence, for early copy editing.

The Minnesota Speculative Fiction Writers Meetup for critique, advice and encouragement.

This has been an
Immortal Production

CPSIA information can be obtained
at www.ICGtesting.com
Printed in the USA
BVHW07s2025021018
529081BV00001B/8/P